Rave Reviews for *The Vagabond*

The Vagabond

The Vagabond

Colette

Translated by Enid McLeod

WINGS BOOKS

New York • Avenel, New Jersey

This 1995 edition is published by Wings Books,
distributed by Random House Value Publishing, Inc.,
40 Engelhard Avenue, Avenel, New Jersey 07001,
by arrangement with Farrar, Straus and Giroux, Inc.

Random House
New York · Toronto · London · Sydney · Auckland

Book design by Kathryn W. Plosica

Printed and bound in the United States of America

Library of Congress Cataloging-in-Publication Data

Colette, 1873–1954.
    [Vagabonde. English]
    The vagabond / Colette ; translated by Enid McLeod.
       p.   cm.
    ISBN 0-517-12259-6
    I. McLeod, Enid.   II. Title.
  PQ2605.028V313   1995
  843'.912—dc20   94-23680
                                                                   CIP

8 7 6 5 4 3 2

Part One

one

TEN THIRTY. . . . ONCE AGAIN I'M READY TOO SOON. MY friend Brague, who helped me when I first began acting in pantomimes, often takes me to task for this in that salty language of his:

"You poor boob of an amateur! You've always got ants in your pants. If we listened to you we'd be putting on our make-up base at half-past seven in the middle of bolting the *hors-d'oeuvre!*"

After three years of music-hall and theatre I'm still the same: always ready too soon.

Ten thirty-five. . . . I'd better open the book lying on the make-up shelf, even though I've read it over and over again, or the copy of *Paris-Sport* the dresser was marking just now with my eyebrow pencil; otherwise I'll find myself all alone, face to face with that painted mentor who gazes at me from the other side of the looking-glass, with deep-set eyes under lids smeared with purplish grease-paint. Her cheek-bones are as brightly coloured as garden phlox and her blackish-red lips gleam as though they were varnished. She gazes at me for a long time and I know she is going to speak to me. She is going to say:

"Is that you there? All alone, there in that cage where idle, impatient, imprisoned hands have scored the white walls with interlaced initials and embellished them with crude, indecent shapes? On those plaster walls reddened nails, like yours, have unconsciously inscribed the appeal of the forsaken. Behind you a feminine hand has carved *Marie*, and the name ends in a passionate mounting flourish, like a cry to heaven. Is it you there, all alone under that ceiling booming and vibrating beneath the feet of the dancers, like the floor of a mill in action? Why are you there, all alone? And why not somewhere else?"

Yes, this is the dangerous, lucid hour. Who will knock at the door of my dressing-room, what face will come between me and the painted mentor peering at me from the other side of the looking-glass? Chance, my master and my friend, will, I feel sure, deign once again to send me the spirits of his unruly kingdom. All my trust is now in him—and in myself. But above all in him, for when I go under he always fishes me out, seizing and shaking me like a life-saving dog whose teeth tear my skin a little every time. So now, whenever I despair, I no longer expect my end, but some bit of luck, some commonplace little miracle which, like a glittering link, will mend again the necklace of my days.

Faith, that is what it is, genuine faith, as blind as it sometimes pretends to be, with all the dissembling renunciations of faith, and that obstinacy which makes it continue to hope even at the moment of crying, "I am utterly forsaken!" There is no doubt that, if ever my heart were to call my master Chance by another name, I should make an excellent Catholic.

How the floor vibrates this evening! It's obvious that it's a cold night: the Russian dancers are warming themselves up! When they all shout "Yoo!" in chorus, in voices as shrill and hoarse as those of young pigs, it will be ten past eleven. My clock is infallible, it does not vary by so much as five minutes in a month. Ten o'clock: I arrive; Mme Cavalier is singing her three songs, *The Little Guttersnipes*, *The Farewell Kiss*, and *The Little You-know-what*. Ten ten: Antonieff and his dogs. Ten twenty-two: shots, barks, end of dog-act. The iron staircase creaks and someone coughs: Jadin is coming down. She swears in the middle of her coughing because she's treading on the hem of her frock; it happens every time. Ten thirty-five: Whimsical Bouty. Ten forty-seven: the Russian dancers, and, finally, eleven ten: me!

Me. As that word came into my head, I involuntarily looked in the mirror. There's no getting away from it, it really is me there behind that mask of purplish rouge, my eyes ringed with a halo of blue grease-paint beginning to melt. Can the rest of my face be going to melt also? What if nothing were to remain from my whole reflection but a streak of dyed colour stuck to the glass like a long, muddy tear?

It's absolutely freezing in here! I rub my hands together, grey with cold under the wet white which is beginning to crack. Good Lord! the radiator pipes are icy; it is Saturday and on Saturdays here they rely on the high-spirited popular audience, rowdy and slightly drunk, to warm the auditorium. No one has given a thought to the artistes' dressing-rooms.

The door shudders under a blow from a fist, which makes my very ears quiver. I open it to my pal Brague, dressed as a swarthy Roumanian bandit, and conscientious as ever.

"You know it's our turn next?"

"Yes I know. And about time too! I'm frozen to death!"

At the top of the iron staircase leading to the stage, the good, dry, dusty warmth wraps me round like a comfortable dirty cloak. While the ever-meticulous Brague keeps an eye on the setting of the scene and sees to the raising of the stage lights—for a sunset effect—I mechanically glue my eye to the luminous peephole in the drop curtain.

There's a grand Saturday house in this favourite local *café-concert*. The auditorium is dark, as the projectors are not strong enough to illuminate it, and you might bet a shilling you would not find a collar from the tenth row of the stalls to the second gallery! A pall of reddish smoke floats over it all, full of the horrible smell of stale tobacco and twopenny cigars smoked too far down. The stage-boxes, on the other hand, look like four flower-stands. It is indeed a fine Saturday house

5
..

but, as little Jadin vigorously puts it: "To hell with the house, I don't get a rake-off on the takings!"

As soon as the first bars of our overture strike up, I feel soothed and ready for anything, grown all of a sudden gay and irresponsible. With my elbows propped on the canvas balcony, I calmly consider the layer of powdered dirt—composed of mud from shoes, dust, hairs of dogs and crushed gum—covering the boards where soon my bare knees will be crawling, and sniff an artificial red geranium. From that moment I no longer belong to myself, and all is well. I know that I shall not fall when I dance, that my heel will not catch in the hem of my skirt, and that when Brague handles me roughly I shall collapse without grazing my elbows or flattening my nose. I shall keep a straight face when I vaguely hear the little scene-shifter making noises like farts behind the wings at the most dramatic moments to make us laugh. The harsh light sustains me, the music governs my gestures, a mysterious discipline controls and protects me. . . . all is well.

All is indeed well! Our dun-coloured Saturday public has rewarded us with an uproar compounded of bravos, catcalls, shrieks and well-meant ribaldries, and I received, plumb on a corner of my mouth, a little bunch of cheap carnations, those anaemic white carnations which the street flower-sellers dip in carmine-tinted water to dye them. I take it home, pinned to the lapel of my jacket; it smells of pepper and wet dog.

I take home also a letter which has just been handed to me:

"*Madame, I was in the first row of the stalls. Your gifts as a mime incline me to think that you must possess others, more special and still more captivating. Give me the pleasure of supping this evening with me.*"

It is signed "Marquis de Fontanges"—yes, it really is—and written from the Café du Delta. What a number of descendants of noble families which one had thought extinct long ago have taken up residence at the Café du Delta! Unlikely as it seems, I can't help suspecting a close relationship between this Marquis de Fontanges and a Comte de Lavallière who, last week, offered me a "five o'clock" in his bachelors' chambers. Commonplace impostures though these are, one can divine in them that romantic admiration for high life, that respect for a title, which lurks in this tough neighbourhood under more than one battered cap.

t w o

As always, I give a great sigh when I close the door of my ground-floor flat behind me. Is it a sigh of weariness, or relaxation, or relief? Or does it spring from the bitterness of solitude? Better not think of it, far better not!

But what on earth is the matter with me tonight? It must be this icy December fog, like particles of frost hanging in the air, quivering in an iridescent halo round the gas lamps and melting on one's lips with a taste of creosote. And besides, this new quarter where I live, looming up all white behind Les Ternes, is enough to discourage both one's eyes and one's spirit.

My street, under the greenish gas at this hour, is a morass of toffee-like, creamy mud—coffee-coloured, maroon and caramel yellow—a sort of crumbling, slushy trifle in which the floating bits of meringue are lumps of concrete. Even my house, the only one in the street, has a sort of "it can't be true" look. But its new walls and thin partitions offer, at a modest rent, a shelter sufficiently comfortable for "ladies on their own" like me.

When you are a "lady on your own", in other words the landlords' abomination, outcast and terror all rolled into one, you take what you find, lodge where you may and put up with newly plastered walls.

The house where I live compassionately shelters quite a colony of "ladies on their own". On the mezzanine floor we have the acknowledged mistress of Young, of Young-

Automobiles; above, the girl-friend, very much "kept", of the Comte de Bravailles; higher up are two fair-haired sisters, both of whom are visited every day by the same man, a very-correct-gentleman-in-industry; higher still a terrible little tart makes as much of a racket night and day as an unleashed fox-terrier, screaming, playing the piano, singing and throwing empty bottles out of the window.

"She's a disgrace to the house," Madame Young-Automobiles said one day.

Finally, on the ground floor, there is myself who neither screams, nor plays the piano, nor even receives gentlemen and still less ladies. The little tart on the fourth floor makes too much noise and I not enough, as the concierge does not fail to remark to me. "It's funny, one never knows whether Madame is there because one doesn't hear her. One would never think she was an artiste!"

What an ugly December night it is! The radiator smells of iodoform, Blandine has forgotten to put my hot-water bottle in my bed, and even my dog is in a bad mood. Grumpy and shivering, she merely casts one black and white glance at me, without leaving her basket. I must say! I don't expect triumphal arches and illuminations, but all the same . . .

No need to search the place, to peer in the corners or look under the bed, there is no one here, no one but myself. What I see in the big looking-glass in my bedroom is no longer the painted image of an itinerant music-hall artiste. It reflects only —myself.

Behold me then, just as I am! This evening I shall not be able to escape the meeting in the long mirror, the soliloquy which I have a hundred times avoided, accepted, fled from, taken up again and broken off. I feel in advance, alas, the uselessness of trying to change the subject. This evening I shall not feel sleepy, and the spell of a book—even a brand-new book with that smell of printers' ink and paper fresh from

9

the press that makes you think of coal and trains and departures—even that spell will not be able to distract me from myself.

Behold me then, just as I am. Alone alone, and for the rest of my life, no doubt. Already alone; it's early for that. When I turned thirty I did not feel cast down because mine is a face that depends on the expression which animates it, the colour of my eyes, and the defiant smile that plays over it—what Marinetti calls my *gaiezza volpina*. But if I look like a fox, it's a fox without guile, which a hen could catch! And a fox without rapacity, one that remembers only the trap and the cage. A gay-looking fox, if you like, but only because the corners of its mouth and eyes look as if they were smiling. A captive fox, tired of dancing to the sound of music.

It is true enough that I do look like a fox. But a slender, pretty fox is not an ugly thing, is it? Brague says too that I look like a rat when I purse my lips and blink my eyelids so as to see better. I see nothing to mind in that.

But how I dislike seeing myself with that drooping mouth and those slack shoulders, the weight of my whole sad body slumped on one leg! My hair hangs dank and lank and in a little while I shall have to brush it for a long time to give it back its shining beaver brown. My eyes are still faintly ringed with blue eye-shadow and there's a wavering trace of red on my nails. It will take me at least fifty good minutes of bathing and grooming to get rid of all that.

It is one o'clock already. What am I waiting for? A smart little lash with the whip to make the obstinate creature go on again. But no one will give it me because . . . because I am alone. How clearly one sees, in that long frame which holds my reflection, that I'm used already to living alone!

No matter what visitor, for a mere tradesman, or even for my charwoman Blandine, I should raise this drooping neck, straighten that slouching hip and clasp those empty hands. But tonight I am so alone.

* * *

Alone! Indeed one might think I was pitying myself for it!

"If you live all alone," said Brague, "it's because you really want to, isn't it?"

Certainly I "really" want to, and in fact I *want* to, quite simply. Only, well . . . there are days when solitude, for someone of my age, is a heady wine which intoxicates you with freedom, others when it is a bitter tonic, and still others when it is a poison which makes you beat your head against the wall.

This evening I would much prefer not to say which it is; all I want is to remain undecided, and not to be able to say whether the shiver which will seize me when I slip between the cold sheets comes from fear or contentment.

Alone . . . and for a long time past. The proof is that I am giving way to the habit of talking to myself and of holding conversations with my dog, and the fire, and my own reflection. It is an idiosyncracy which recluses and old prisoners fall into; but I'm not like them, I'm free. And if I talk to myself it is because I have a writer's need to express my thoughts in rhythmical language.

Facing me from the other side of the looking-glass, in that mysterious reflected room, is the image of "a woman of letters who has turned out badly". They also say of me that I'm "on the stage", but they never call me an actress. Why? The nuance is subtle, but there is certainly a polite refusal, on the part both of the public and my friends themselves, to accord me any standing in this career which I have nevertheless adopted. A woman of letters who has turned out badly: that is what I must remain for everyone, I who no longer write, who deny myself the pleasure, the luxury of writing.

To write, to be able to write, what does it mean? It means spending long hours dreaming before a white page, scribbling unconsciously, letting your pen play round a blot of ink and nibble at a half-formed word, scratching it, making it bristle with darts and adorning it with antennae and paws until it loses all resemblance to a legible word and turns into a fantastic insect or a fluttering creature half butterfly, half fairy.

To write is to sit and stare, hypnotised, at the reflection of the window in the silver ink-stand, to feel the divine fever mounting to one's cheeks and forehead while the hand that writes grows blissfully numb upon the paper. It also means idle hours curled up in the hollow of the divan, and then the orgy of inspiration from which one emerges stupefied and aching all over, but already recompensed and laden with treasures that one unloads slowly on to the virgin page in the little round pool of light under the lamp.

To write is to pour one's innermost self passionately upon the tempting paper, at such frantic speed that sometimes one's hand struggles and rebels, overdriven by the impatient god who guides it—and to find, next day, in place of the golden bough that bloomed miraculously in that dazzling hour, a withered bramble and a stunted flower.

To write is the joy and torment of the idle. Oh to write! From time to time I feel a need, sharp as thirst in summer, to note and to describe. And then I take up my pen again and attempt the perilous and elusive task of seizing and pinning down, under its flexible double-pointed nib, the many-hued, fugitive, thrilling adjective. . . . The attack does not last long; it is but the itching of an old scar.

It takes up too much time to write. And the trouble is, I am no Balzac! The fragile story I am constructing crumbles away when the tradesman rings, or the shoemaker sends in his bill, when the solicitor, or one's counsel, telephones, or when the theatrical agent summons me to his office for "a social engagement at the house of some people of very good position but not in the habit of paying large fees".

The problem is, since I have been living alone, that I have had first to live, then to divorce, and then to go on living. To do all that demands incredible activity and persistence. And to get where? Is there, for me, no other haven than this commonplace room done up in gimcrack Louis XVI? Must I stay for ever before this impenetrable mirror where I come up against myself, face to face?

Tomorrow is Sunday: that means afternoon and evening performances at the *Empyrée-Clichy*. Two o'clock already! High time for a woman of letters who has turned out badly to go to sleep.

three

"LOOK ALIVE, FOR HEAVEN'S SAKE, LOOK ALIVE! JADIN'S NOT here!"

"How d'you mean, not here? Is she ill?"

"Ill? I'll say! On the spree, more like. The result's the same for us: we go on twenty minutes sooner!"

The mime Brague has just emerged from his dressing-room as I pass, a frightening sight under his khaki-coloured make-up base, and I rush to my dressing-room, full of dismay at the thought that, for the first time in my life, I may be late.

Jadin's not here! I hurry, trembling with nerves, for you can't trifle with our local public, especially at a Sunday mati-née. If, as our wild-beast tamer of a stage-manager says, we let it "get hungry" for five minutes between two acts, hootings and cigarette ends and orange peel automatically begin to fly.

Jadin not here! We might have known it would happen one of these days.

Jadin is a little singer, so new to the *café-concert* that she has not yet had time to peroxide her light brown hair; she came straight to the stage from the outer boulevards, flabbergasted at being able to earn two hundred and ten francs a month by singing. She is eighteen. Luck—should one call it?—immedi-ately got her in its grip, and everything about her, the elbows with which she defends herself and her whole obstinate person bent forward like a gargoyle, looks as if it were warding off the blows of a brutal and fraudulent fate.

She sings like a little seamstress or a street singer, and it never occurs to her that there is any other way of singing. In her artless way she forces her harsh, seductive contralto which goes so well with her face, the face of a pink and sulky young apache. The public adores her just as she is, with her dress that is too long and bought goodness knows where, her light brown hair not even waved, her hunched shoulder which looks as if it were still lugging along the laundry basket, and the down on her upper lip all white with cheap powder. The manageress promises her, for next season, her name in lights twice over, and as for a raise—well we'll see, after that. When she is on the stage Jadin is radiant and exultant. Every evening she recognises, among the public of the upper galleries, some pal of a childish escapade, and she can never resist interrupting her sentimental ditty to greet him with a joyful shout, a shrill schoolgirl laugh or even a resounding slap on her thigh.

And this is the girl who is missing from today's programme. In half an hour they will be rampaging in the house, calling "Jadin! Jadin!", stamping their boots and rattling their mazagran spoons against their glasses.

It was bound to happen. Jadin, they say, is not ill, and our stage-manager grumbles:

" 'Flu, my foot! She's come a cropper into a bed, that's what she's done! And someone's using his wallet as a compress to keep her there! Otherwise she'd have let us know."

Jadin has found a fancier who does not belong to this district. A girl must live. But she was living already, with Tom, Dick and Harry. Shall I ever again see her little gargoyle silhouette, with one of those "modish" forage caps she used to fabricate herself, coming right down to her eyebrows? Only last night she thrust her badly-powdered little mug into my dressing-room to show me her latest creation: an "imitation white fox" toque of rabbit fur, so tight fitting that it pressed her little pink ears down on each side.

"You look the dead spit of Attila," Brague told her, with never a smile.

And now she's gone. The long corridor, perforated with

little square dressing-rooms, buzzes with derisive laughter: it seems that everyone except me suspected this flight. Bouty, the little funny-man who sings the songs that Dranem made famous, walks up and down outside my dressing-room, made up like an ape, with a glass of milk in his hand, and I hear him prophesying: "It was a cert! But I couldn't help thinking Jadin would hold out another five or six days, or even a month! The boss must be livid! But it'll take more than that to make her decide to raise the screw of us artistes who make the reputation of her house for her. Just you mark my words: we'll be seeing Jadin back again; it's only a jaunt, that's all. She's a girl who knows where she belongs, she'll never be able to keep a fancy chap."

I open my door to speak to Bouty while I am putting the wet white on my hands: "Didn't she tell you she was going away, Bouty?"

He shrugs his shoulders, turning towards me his red gorilla mask, with its white-rimmed eyes: "Not likely! I'm not her mother." Whereupon he starts gulping his glass of milk, as blue as starch, in little sips.

Poor little Bouty, trailing about with him everywhere his chronic enteritis and his bottle of tested milk! When he removes that white and vermilion mask he reveals a gentle, sickly face, delicate and intelligent, with beautiful tender eyes, and the heart of an ownerless dog ready to devote itself to anyone who will adopt it. His illness and his exacting profession are killing him, he lives on milk and boiled macaroni, and has just enough strength to sing and dance Negro dances for twenty minutes. When he leaves the set he falls exhausted in the wings, unable immediately to go down to his dressing-room. Sometimes his slender body, stretched out there as if dead, bars my way, and I have to harden myself not to stoop and pick him up and call for help. His fellow actors and the old stage-setter content themselves with shaking their heads with an important air as they pass him, and saying: "Bouty's an artist who 'tires' quickly."

16

* * *

"Come on now, we must get a move on, full speed ahead! The house didn't yell for Jadin as much as they might. That's a bit of luck for us!"

Brague hustles me up the iron staircase: the combination of dusty heat and stage-lighting makes me dizzy; this matinée has been like one of those dreams full of incident, half the day has melted away I don't know how, leaving me with nothing but the kind of nervous chill and contraction of the stomach which follow awakenings and rapid risings in the middle of the night. In an hour it will be time for dinner, then a taxi, and it starts all over again.

And that's how it will be for a month! The present show is quite a success and anyhow we must keep it going until the *Revue* begins.

"We're in clover here," says Brague. "Forty days with nothing to think about!"

With nothing to think about. . . . If only I could do as he does! I've got forty days, the whole year, a lifetime for thinking in. How long am I going to spend trailing round, from music-hall to theatre, and from theatre to casino, "gifts" that everyone politely agrees to consider interesting? They admit in addition that my mimicry is "exact", my diction "clear", and my figure "impeccable". It's very kind of them. It goes even beyond what is necessary. But . . . where does it lead?

It's no good, I can see I'm in for a bad fit of the blues. I await it calmly, with a heart that is used to it, knowing I shall recognise its normal phases and get the better of it once again. No one will know anything about it. This evening Brague gives me a quizzical look with his penetrating little eyes, but merely says: "Wool-gathering, aren't you?"

17

Back in my dressing-room I wash my hands, stained red-currant colour to simulate blood, in front of the looking-glass where my painted mentor and I gravely take stock of each other like well-matched adversaries.

I know there's no escaping what's coming: suffering,

regrets, and the insomnia and solitary musings that make the deepest hours of the night longer still. So I go to meet it with a kind of grim gaiety, and with all the serenity of a creature still young and resistant, who has been through it before. Two habits have taught me how to keep back my tears: the habit of concealing my thoughts, and that of darkening my lashes with mascara. . . .

"Come in!"

Someone has just knocked and I answered mechanically, my thoughts elsewhere.

It is neither Brague nor the old dresser, but an unknown person, tall, gaunt and dark, who bows his bare head announces, without pausing for breath: "Every night this week, Madame, I have come here to applaud you in *The Pursuit*. If my visit appears to you somewhat . . . out of place I hope you will forgive it, but I feel that my admiration for your talent and . . . your figure . . . is sufficient excuse for my presenting myself so . . . unconventionally and that . . ."

I do not answer this imbecile. Damp with sweat and still out of breath, with my dress half undone, I look at him, while I wipe my hands, with such evident ferocity that his fine phrases falter and die suddenly on his lips.

Ought I to slap his face and leave on both cheeks the marks of my fingers still wet with carmine-tinted water? Ought I to raise my voice and hurl at the angular, bony face, barred with a black moustache, the words I have learnt behind the scenes and in the street?

He has the eyes of a sad coal-miner, this intruder. I have no idea how he interprets my look and my silence, but all of a sudden his expression changes.

"Oh my goodness, Madame, what a clumsy creature I am, nothing but a noodle and I've only just realised it. Turn me out, do, I've richly deserved it, but not before I've laid my respectful compliments at your feet."

He bows once more, like a man who is just about to go—and does not go. With that somewhat harlot-like artfulness that men have, he waits for half a second to see if his changed approach may have brought him any reward and—after all I'm not so terrible—it has.

"Well then, Monsieur, I will say to you politely what a moment ago I would have said harshly: please go!"

As I show him the door I laugh in a jolly way. But he does not laugh. He remains where he is, craning forward, his free hand hanging down with the fist clenched. In this attitude he looks awkward and almost menacing, with the slightly clumsy air of a wood-cutter on his best behaviour. The ceiling light is reflected in his sleek, almost lacquered-looking black hair brushed back at the sides; but his eyes are so deep set I cannot see their expression.

The reason why he does not laugh is because he desires me. He does not want my well-being, this man, he merely wants me. He is not in a mood for jests, even smutty ones. In the end this makes me uncomfortable and I would prefer him to be unashamedly lustful, like a man who has dined well and thoroughly enjoyed an eyeful in the front row of the stalls.

He is as hampered by his ardent desire for me as if it were a weapon getting in his way.

"Well, Monsieur, aren't you going?"

His answer bursts out as if I had awakened him: "Of course, of course, Madame! Certainly I'm going. I beg you to accept my excuses and . . ."

". . . and believe me to be your humble servant!" I could not help ending.

It is not very funny, but he laughs, at last he laughs, and changes that obstinate expression which I had found so disconcerting.

"It's kind of you to help me out, Madame! There's another thing too I wanted to ask you . . ."

"Oh, no, you don't, you're going right away this minute.

I've been amazingly long-suffering with you already, and if I don't soon take off this dress, after sweating in it like three furniture-removers, I shall get bronchitis!"

I push him out with the tip of my first finger, for as soon as I spoke of taking off my dress his face went dark and set again. Even after the door is shut and bolted, I can hear his muffled voice begging: "Madame! Madame! I wanted to know if you like flowers, and if so which ones?"

"Monsieur! Monsieur! leave me in peace! I don't ask you which are your favourite poets or if you prefer the sea to the mountains. Go away!"

"I'm going, Madame! Good evening, Madame!"

Ouf! This great noodle of a man has driven away my black mood; that is something at any rate.

For the last three years my amorous conquests have all been like this. The gentleman in the eleventh stall, the gentleman in the fourth box, the gigolo in the upper circle. A letter, two letters, a bouquet, another letter . . . and that's the end of it. Silence soon discourages them and I have to admit to myself that they are not overpersistent.

Fate, by way of sparing my energies for the future, seems to keep away from me those obstinate lovers, those hunters who pursue a woman until she physically does not know which way to turn. Those whom I attract do not write me love letters. Their letters are urgent, brutal and awkward, betraying their desires, not their thoughts. The one exception was a wretched youth who covered twelves pages with his abashed and garrulous love. He must have been very young. He used to dream of himself as a Prince Charming, poor lad, rich and powerful too: "I am writing you all this at the table in a pub where I'm having my lunch, and every time I raise my head I see my ugly mug in the looking-glass opposite."

At least that little admirer with the "ugly mug", lost in his azure palaces and enchanted forests, could dream of someone. But there is no one waiting for me on the road I follow, a road leading neither to glory nor riches nor love. Not that anything, as I well know, leads to love. It is love who throws himself across your path. And then he either blocks it for ever or, if he abandons it, leaves it in rack and ruin.

What remains of my life reminds me of the pieces of a jigsaw puzzle. Have I got to try and reconstruct, piece by piece, the original scene of it: a quiet house in the middle of a wood? No, no, I can't, someone has jumbled together all the outlines of that sweet landscape; I should never even be able to find again the bits of the blue roof patterned with yellow lichen, nor the virginia creeper, nor the deep forest without birds. . . .

Eight years of marriage and three of separation: that accounts for a third of my whole existence.

My ex-husband? You all knew him, Adolphe Taillandy, the pastellist. He has been doing the same portrait of a woman for the last twenty years. She is always in evening dress, posed against a misty gold background borrowed from Lévy-Dhurmer, and her hair, like floss silk, forms a halo round the velvety bloom of her face. The flesh on her temples, in the shadow of her neck, and between the swelling curves of her breasts, glows with the same impalpable bloom, the dusky blue of luscious grapes which tempt one's lips.

"Even Potel and Chabot can't improve on it!" said Forain one day before a pastel of my husband's.

Apart from his famous "bloom" I do not think that Adolphe Taillandy has any talent. But I freely admit that his portraits are irresistible, especially to women. To begin with, he resolutely sees everything in a rosy light. He has even found—goodness knows where—some red and golden glints to beautify the hair of that withered and superannuated brunette, Madame de Guimont-Fautru. These flecks of light, scattered over her lustreless face and Greek nose turn her into a voluptuous Venetian courtesan.

Once upon a time Taillandy did my portrait too. No one now remembers that I was the model for his picture of the

21
.....

little bacchante with the shiny nose, where a splash of sunlight, falling full on her face, makes it look like a mask of mother-of-pearl. I still remember my surprise at finding myself so blonde. I remember, too, the success of this pastel and of those which followed it. There were the portraits of Mme de Guimont-Fautru, of Baroness Avelot, of Mme de Chalis, of Mme Robert-Durand, and of the singer Jane Doré. Then we come to those which were less illustrious because of the anonymity of the sitters: the portraits of Mlle J.R., of Mlle S.S., of Mme U., of Mme Van O., and of Mrs. F.W.

That was the period when Adolphe Taillandy used to declare, with that typical effrontery of the handsome man which became him so well: "I want no models but my mistresses, and no mistresses but my models!"

As far as I am concerned, the only genius he had was for lying. No woman, none of his women, could possibly have appraised and admired, feared and cursed his passion for lying as much as I did. Adolphe Taillandy used to lie feverishly, voluptuously, untiringly, almost involuntarily. For him, adultery was merely a type of falsehood, and by no means the most delectable.

He luxuriated in lies, with a strength and prodigality that was undiminished by the passing years. And while he was busy elaborating some ingenious piece of perfidy, designed with infinite care and embellished with all the studied refinements at the command of this arch-deceiver, I would see him squandering his passion for cunning in crude and vulgar deceptions that were quite unnecessary, and stories that were childish to the point of imbecility.

22

I met him, married him, lived with him for eight years . . . and what do I know of him? That he paints pastels and has mistresses. I know, too, that he achieves daily the disconcerting feat of being, for one person, a "plodder" who thinks of nothing but his art; for one woman a seductive and unscrupulous ruffian; for another a fatherly lover who seasons a passing infatuation with a piquant flavour of incest; for still another the tired, disillusioned and aging artist seeking to adorn his autumn with a delicate idyll. There is even the woman for whom he is, quite simply, an unchartered libertine, still vigorous and as lecherous as could be desired; and finally there is the silly little goose, well brought up and deeply enamoured, whom Adolphe Taillandy taunts, torments, spurns and takes back again with all the literary cruelty of an "artist" in a society novel.

This same Taillandy slips without transition into the no less conventional but more old-fashioned "artist" who, in order to overcome the last resistance of the little woman who is married and the mother of two children, throws down his chalks, tears up his sketch, weeps real tears which wet his Kaiser-like moustache and, seizing his broad-brimmed felt, rushes off to the waters of the Seine.

There are still many more Taillandys whom I shall never know, not to mention one of the most shocking: Taillandy in his business dealings, the shady juggler in money matters who is brazen and brutal, or smooth and shifty as occasion demands.

Among all those men which is the real one? I humbly declare that I have no idea. I believe there is no *real* Taillandy. There came a day when this prolific genius of a liar suddenly lost the power to make me despair and even ceased to interest me. Time was when he had been for me a sort of terrifying Machiavelli; perhaps after all he was only Fregoli.

In any case he still continues as before. There are times when I think of his second wife with a faint compassion. Is she still in love and blissfully savouring what she calls her victory over me? No, by this time, terrified and helpless, she must be beginning to find out what manner of man she has married.

Sometimes I sigh: "Heavens, how young I was and how I loved that man! And how I suffered!" But when I do, it is not at all a cry of pain or vengeful lamentation. It is rather as

23

though I were saying: "If you knew how ill I was four years ago!" And when I admit: "I've been jealous to the point of wanting to kill, and die", I do it in the same way as those people who tell you: "I ate rats in '70!" They remember they did, but the memory of it is all they have. They know they ate rats, but they can no longer conjure up in themselves the shiver of horror, nor the anguish of famine.

After the first betrayals, the revolts and submissions of a youthful love determined to hope and to endure, I settled down to suffering with an unyielding pride and obstinacy, and to producing literature.

Just for the pleasure of taking refuge in a still recent past, I wrote *The Ivy on the Wall*, a cheerful little provincial novel, as clear and unruffled as the pools in my part of the world, a chaste little novel of love and marriage, slightly insipid and very agreeable, which had an unexpected and extravagant success. I found my photo in all the illustrated papers, *Life Today* awarded me its annual prize, and Adolphe and I became "the most interesting couple in Paris", the couple one invites to dinner and points out to distinguished foreigners. "You don't know the Taillandys? Renée Taillandy is extremely gifted." "Really? And what about him?" "He? Oh, he's irresistible!"

My second book, *Next Door to Love*, did not sell nearly as well. Yet in giving birth to it I had savoured the voluptuous pleasure of writing, the patient struggling with a phrase until it becomes supple and finally settles down, curled up like a tamed animal, the motionless lying in wait for a word by which in the end one *ensnares* it. Yes, my second volume sold very little. But it managed to win me the—what is the expression one uses? oh yes, of course—"the esteem of the literary world". As for the third, *The Forest Without Birds*, it fell flat and never picked up again. Yet this one is my favourite, my private "unrecognised masterpiece". It was considered diffuse and muddled, incomprehensible and long. Even now, whenever I open it, I love it and wholeheartedly admire myself in it.

Incomprehensible? Perhaps it is for you. But for me its warm obscurity is clear as day; for me a single word is enough to create again the smell and colour of hours I have lived through. It is as sonorous and full of mystery as a shell in which the sea sings, and I should love it less, I think, if you loved it too. But rest assured, I shall not write another like that, I never could.

At present other tasks and cares fill my time, especially that of earning my living, bartering my gestures, my dances and the sound of my voice for hard cash. I have got very quickly into the way of that and enjoy it, having a characteristically feminine fondness for money. And earn my living I certainly do. On my good days I joyfully say over and over again to myself that I earn my living. The music-hall where I became mime, dancer and even on occasion, actress, turned me also, despite my astonishment at finding myself reckoning, haggling and bargaining, into a tough but honest little business woman. The least gifted of women soon learns how to be that when her life and liberty depend upon it.

No one could understand our separation at all. But would anyone in the least have understood my patience and my utter complacency, so cowardly and long-lasting, before it came to that? It is, alas, only the first forgiveness which is difficult. Adolphe soon learnt that I belonged to the true, the best breed of females: in other words, that I was the kind of woman who, having forgiven on the first occasion, can gradually and cleverly be let to become one who submits and then finally accepts. What an expert master I had in him! How skilfully he alternated between indulgence and exigence! When I showed myself too intractable he even went so far as to beat me, though I believe he never really wanted to do that. A man who has lost his temper does not beat as well as he did, and he only struck me from time to time to keep up his prestige. At the time of our divorce the world was almost ready to lay all the blame on me, in order to exculpate "that good-looking Taillandy", whose only fault was that he was attractive and faithless. I was within an inch of giving in and letting myself be intimidated and reduced to my habitual submissiveness by the turmoil which the whole thing created around us.

"D'you mean to say that he's been deceiving her for eight years and it's only now that she's thought of complaining?"

I received visits from domineering friends, superior persons who know "what life is"; and others from aged relations whose most serious argument was: "What do you expect, my dear child!"

What did I expect? At bottom I knew very well. I had had enough of it. What did I want? To die, rather than prolong that humiliating life of a woman "who has everything to make her happy"; to die, yes, and risk misery before suicide, but never again to see Adolphe Taillandy, the Adolphe Taillandy who only showed himself in domestic privacy, the one who, without raising his voice, thrusting that formidable adjutant's chin of his towards me, knew so well how to warn me: "Tomorrow I'm beginning the portrait of Mme Mothier. You'll be good enough, I am sure, to take that expression off your face in future when you're looking at her."

To die, risking utter ruin first, but never again to surprise the sudden gesture which conceals a crumpled letter, nor the falsely commonplace conversation on the telephone, nor the glance of the servant who is in the know, and never again to hear myself told in a casual tone: "Oughtn't you to go and stay with your mother for a couple of days this week?"

To go away, but never again to lower myself to taking one of my husband's mistresses out for a walk all day, while he, reassured and protected by me, was embracing another. To go away, and die, but no longer to pretend ignorance, no longer to endure the nightly waiting, the vigil when one's feet grow cold in the too-big bed, no longer to think out those plans for vengeance which, born in the dark and inflated by the beatings of a lacerated heart, poisoned by jealousy, collapse at the rattle of a key in the lock and feebly let themselves be mollified when a familiar voice cries: "What? Not asleep yet?"

I had had enough.

You can get used to not eating, to having toothache or a pain in your stomach, you can even get used to the absence of a beloved person; but you cannot get used to jealousy. And so there happened what Adolphe Taillandy, who thinks of everything, had not foreseen: one day when without courtesy he had shown me *my own* door, so that he might better entertain Mme Mothier on the big divan in the studio, I did not return.

I returned neither that night, nor the next, nor on any night thereafter. And that is where my story ends—or begins.

I will not dwell on a short and gloomy period of transition during which I received, with the same peevish humour, blame, advice, sympathy and even congratulations.

I discouraged the few persistent friends who came and rang at the door of a tiny flat I had chanced to rent. I felt so outraged to think that, in order to see me, anyone should appear to be defying that sacrosanct, all-powerful and vile thing, public opinion, that I severed, with a furious gesture, the last remaining links that still bound me to my past.

And what followed? Isolation? Yes, isolation, except for three or four friends, obstinate, burr-like creatures who had resolved to put up with all my rebuffs. How ill I received them, but how I loved them, and how frightened I was, when I watched them go, that they might not come again.

Isolation indeed. I was scared of it, as of a remedy which may kill. And then I discovered that all I was doing was to go on living alone. My training in that had begun long ago, in my childhood, and the first years of my marriage had barely interrupted it. Then it had started anew, severe this time and harsh enough to draw tears; and that is the most ordinary part of my story. What numbers of women have experienced that retreat into themselves, that patient withdrawal which follows their rebellious tears! I will do them this justice, which flatters me too: it is only in pain that a woman is capable of rising above mediocrity. Her resistance to pain is infinite; one can use and abuse it without any fear that she will die, as long as some childish physical cowardice or some religious hope keeps her from the suicide that offers a way out.

"She is dying of grief. . . . She has died of grief. . . ." When you hear those clichés you can shake your head, more in disbelief than compassion: a woman can never die of grief. She is such a solid creature, so hard to kill! You think that grief eats into her? Not at all. Very often, though born weak and sickly, she gains from grief indestructible nerves, an inflexible pride, a capacity for waiting and dissimulating which increases her stature, and a contempt for those who are happy. She grows supple in the practice of suffering and dissimulation, as if they were daily exercises full of risks. For she is always on the verge of that keenest and sweetest and most seductive of all temptations, the temptation of revenge.

Sometimes, if she is too weak or too loving, she kills. And when that happens she will be able to astonish the whole world with an example of that disconcerting feminine resistance. Like a cunning animal leading on inexperienced dogs, she will wear out her judges in the course of interminable sessions and finally leave them exhausted. You can be certain that long patience, and griefs jealously hidden have tempered and sharpened and toughened this woman till everyone cries "She's made of steel!" No, she is merely made "of woman"— and that is enough.

Solitude, freedom, my pleasant and painful work as mime and dancer, tired and happy muscles, and, by way of a change from all that, the new anxiety about earning my meals, my clothes, and my rent—such, all of a sudden, was my lot. But with it too went a savage defiance, a disgust for the milieu where I had lived and suffered, a stupid fear of man, of men, and of women too. I felt a morbid need to ignore what was happening round me, to have near me none but rudimentary creatures who would hardly think at all. Very quickly, too, there came to me that odd sensation that only on the stage was I really alone and safe from my fellow-creatures, protected from the whole world by the barrier of light.

four

SUNDAY AGAIN! BUT NOW THE MURKY COLD HAS GIVEN PLACE to a bright cold, so we have taken our exercise, my dog and I, in the Bois between eleven and twelve. There is a matinée after lunch. The creature is ruining me. If it were not for her I could get to the Bois in the Metro, but she gives me pleasure in return for my three francs on the taxi. Black as a truffle, polished with a brush and a flannel rag, she gleams in the sun; the whole wood is hers and she takes possession of it, grunting like a pig and barking as she scatters the dry leaves.

How lovely it is, the Bois de Boulogne on a fine Sunday! For Fossette and me, city tramps who hardly know the country now, it is our forest and our park. Fossette runs faster than I do, but I walk faster than she does, and when she is not playing at "inner circle" with mad bulging eyes and her tongue hanging out, she bounds along after me in short rushes of little trotting gallops which make everyone laugh.

One can gaze full at the tarnished sun because its light is filtered by a fine rosy mist. A quivering, silvery incense, smelling faintly of mushrooms, rises from the open stretches of grass. My veil clings to my nose as I rush along, my whole body glowing with running and tingling with the cold. Am I in truth any different from what I was at twenty? On such a winter morning as this, surely even in the full flower of adolescence I was neither more firm nor more supple nor more sensually happy?

I can believe it as long as I am running through the Bois,

but when I return home my fatigue undeceives me. It is no longer the *same* fatigue. When I was twenty I should have enjoyed my temporary lassitude, sunk in a half-dream without any mental reserves. But nowadays I begin to find fatigue irksome, like a sort of bodily distress.

Fossette is a born luxury-dog and play-actress: the *boards* thrill her and she has a craze for jumping into every elegant car she sees. Yet it was Stephen-the-Dancer who sold her to me, and at no time did Fossette ever belong to a successful actress. Stephen-the-Dancer is one of my comrades working at the moment in the same "dump", the *Empyrée-Clichy*. A prey to tuberculosis which year by year is eating him up, this fair Gaul witnesses the gradual dissolution of his biceps, his rosy thighs gleaming with golden down, and the beautiful chest muscles of which he is so justly proud. Already he has had to give up boxing for dancing and roller-skating. He *rinks* here on the sloping stage; in addition he has set up as a dancing teacher, and on the side he also breeds domestic bulldogs. This winter he is coughing a great deal. Often in the evenings he comes to my dressing-room, coughs, sits down and suggests that I should buy "a brindled, grey, bulldog bitch, a perfect beauty, who missed the first prize this year because of some jealousy".

It so happens that I arrive today in the underground corridor, honey-combed with square cells, which leads to my dressing-room, just at the moment when Stephen-the-Dancer is leaving the stage. With his slender waist, broad shoulders, tight-fitting Polish dolman of myrtle-green edged with imitation chinchilla, and fur cap over one ear, the young man still draws the eyes of the women, with his blue eyes and slightly rouged cheeks. But he is getting slowly thinner and thinner and his successes with women hasten his disease.

"Hullo!"

"Hullo, Stephen! Good house?"

"I'll say! But I can't think why the buzzards muck around here when it's so lovely in the country. By the way you don't happen to need a schipperke bitch who weighs just over a pound—a bargain I could get hold of through an acquaintance . . ."

"Just over a pound! Thanks, my flat's too small!"

He immediately laughs and does not insist. I know them well, those schipperke bitches, weighing just over a pound, that Stephen sells. They weigh round about six pounds. It is not dishonesty, it is business.

What will Stephen-the-Dancer do when he's down to his last lung, when he can't dance any more or sleep any longer with kind-hearted little women who buy him cigars, ties and drinks? What hospital, what institution will take in his beautiful hollow carcass? How far from funny all that is! And indeed what a lot of people there are whose misery doesn't bear thinking of!

"Hullo, Bouty! Hullo, Brague! Any news of Jadin?"

Brague shrugs his shoulders without answering, so intent is he on the tricky job of making up his eyebrows; he paints them dark violet because "that gives a fiercer look". He has a particular blue for wrinkles, a particular orangy-red for the inside of lips, a particular ochre for make-up base, a particular syrupy carmine for dripping blood, and above all a particular white for Pierrot masks, "the recipe for which", he avers, "I wouldn't give to my own brother!" There's no denying that he makes a very skilful use of this multi-coloured mania of his, and it is the only absurdity I know of in this intelligent, almost over-conscientious pantomimist.

Bouty, looking skinnier than ever in his loose checked garment, makes a mysterious sign to me. "I say, I've seen that kid Jadin. I saw her on the boulevard, with a bloke. She had feathers like that! And a muff like that! And a look as though she was bored to death at the rate of a pound a minute!"

"Well, if she's getting a pound a minute she's got nothing to complain of," interrupts Brague, always logical.

"I didn't say she was, old chap. But she won't stay on the

boulevard; she's a girl who has no idea of money. I've kept my eye on Jadin for a long time, I have; she and her mother used to live in my court. . . ."

From my open dressing-room opposite that of Brague, I can see little Bouty, who has suddenly fallen silent in the middle of his sentence. He has put his half-litre of tested milk to warm on the hot-water pipe which runs through the dressing-rooms just above floor level. You can't make out much of his real face behind the brick-red and chalk-white mask of his make-up; but I can't help thinking that, since Jadin's departure, poor little Bouty is more wretched than ever.

When I get to the stage of whitening and powdering my shoulders, and my knees which are a mass of bruises—for Brague is not exactly gentle when he throws me to the ground —I close the door, feeling sure in any case that Bouty will say no more. Like the rest of them, and myself too, he hardly ever speaks of his private life. It was this silence, this obstinate modesty, which gave me the wrong impression of his comrades during my early days at the music-hall. The most expansive and the vainest of them talk of their successes and their artistic ambitions with the emphasis and gravity that their code demands; the most malicious go as far as running down the "dump" and their pals; the most talkative are always repeating old stage and green-room jokes; but only one in ten feels the need to say: "I've got a wife—I've got two kids—my mother's ill—I'm awfully worried about my girl friend. . . ."

This silence about their private lives seems like a polite way of saying: "The rest is no concern of yours!" As soon as they have removed their grease-paint and put on their hats and scarves, they separate and disappear with a promptitude which I like to think comes as much from pride as discretion. Proud they nearly all are, and poor: the pal who is always bumming a loan is an exception in the music-hall. My silent sympathy, which has been making discoveries and learning during these last three years, goes out to all of them without any preferences.

33

How unrecognised they are, these *café-concert artistes*, how disparaged and how little understood! Fanciful, proud, and full of an absurd and outmoded faith in Art, they are the only people left who still dare to assert with passionate belief "An *artiste* must not . . . an *artiste* cannot accept . . . an *artiste* will not consent . . ." Proud they certainly are, for though they often exclaim: "Lousy job, ours!" or "What a dog's life!", I have never heard one of them sigh "How unhappy I am!"

Proud, and resigned to existing for only one hour in the twenty-four since, even when it applauds them, the unjust public forgets them afterwards. A newspaper may enquire with discreet solicitude into the way Mlle X. of the *Comédie Fran-çaise* spends her time, and beguile the leisure hours of the whole world with her opinions on fashion, politics, cooking and love; but who will condescend to wonder what you do, poor intelligent, sensitive little Bouty, and what you think and do not say when darkness has swallowed you up and you are hurrying, towards midnight, along the Boulevard Rochechouart, so thin you are almost transparent in your long "English style" overcoat, which comes from the Samaritaine?

For the twentieth time I ponder, all alone to myself, on these things that are so far from cheerful. And while I do so my fingers briskly and unconsciously perform their accustomed task: white grease, pink grease, powder, dry rose, blue, brown, red, black. . . . I have barely finished when a hard claw scratches the bottom of my door. I open at once because it is the begging paw of a little Brabançon terrier who "has a part" in the first half of the show.

"Hullo, Nelle!"

In she comes, confident and as grave as a trusted employee, and lets me pat her little flanks, hot with exercise, while her teeth, slightly yellowed with age, crumble a biscuit. Nelle has a gleaming sandy coat, with a face like a black marmoset's, in which shine beautiful squirrel's eyes.

"Want another biscuit, Nelle?"

Well brought up, she accepts without a smile. Behind her,

in the corridor, her family is waiting for her. Her family consists of a tall, lean man, silent and impenetrable, who speaks to no one, and two courteous white collies who look very much like their master. Where does he come from? What paths have led him and his collies here, like three disinherited princes? His gestures, his way of raising his hat, his long hatchet face—everything about him suggests a man of the world. It was perhaps some gift of divination which made my comrades christen him "the Archduke".

He waits in the corridor till Nelle has finished her biscuit. Nothing could be sadder, more dignified or more disdainful than this man and his three creatures, proudly resigned to their wandering lot.

"Goodbye, Nelle."

I close the door and the tinklings of the little dog's bell grow faint. Shall I see her again? A fortnight's programme comes to an end this evening and perhaps it is the end of an engagement for "Antonieff and his dogs". Where will they go next? Where will Nelle's beautiful brown eyes be shining, those eyes which say to me so clearly: "Yes, I know, you fondle me, you love me, you keep a box of biscuits for me. But to-morrow, or the day after, we shall leave. So don't expect any more of me than the civility of a nice little dog who knows how to walk on her front paws and perform a risky jump. Tenderness, like rest and security, is for us an inaccessible luxury."

f i v e

IN BRIGHT WEATHER MY GROUND FLOOR, BETWEEN ITS TWO cliffs of new houses, enjoys a shaft of sunshine from eight in the morning until two in the afternoon. First a glittering pencil touches my bed, then it spreads out there like a square cloth of light and the coverlet throws a pink reflection up to the ceiling.

I wait, lazily, until the sunlight reaches my face, dazzling me through my closed eyelids, and the shadow of each pedestrian passes swiftly over me like a dark blue wing. Or perhaps, roused to action, I jump out of bed and begin some feverish scouring: Fossette's ears undergo a delicate probing and her coat gleams under the hard brush. Or perhaps I take advantage of the brilliant, pitiless light to inspect what is already showing signs of age in me: the delicate silk of my eyelids, the corner of my mouth where my smile has already begun to engrave a sad line, and round my throat that triple necklace of Venus which an invisible hand presses a little more deeply into my flesh every day.

Today this severe examination is interrupted by the visit of my comrade Brague, brisk, sober and on the spot as usual. I receive him as I do in my dressing-room, with nothing on but a crêpe kimono on which Fossette's paws, one rainy day, printed some little grey, four-petalled flowers.

No need to powder my nose for Brague, nor to lengthen my eyelids with blue pencil. Brague never looks at me except at rehearsals, to say "Don't do that: it's ugly. Don't open your mouth vertically: you look like a fish. Don't blink your eyes: you look like a white rat. Don't wobble your behind when you walk: you look like a mare."

It was Brague who guided, if not my first steps, at least my first gestures on the stage; and if I still show him the trust of a pupil, he for his part often continues to treat me as an "intelligent amateur", by which I mean that he is slightly impatient of discussion and considers that his opinion ought to prevail.

As he comes in this morning he plasters his hair against his neck as though he were pulling down a wig; and since that alert but sober expression, so characteristic of his clean-shaven, Catalan face, remains unchanged, I begin to wonder whether it is good news he is bringing, or bad. He eyes my ray of sunshine as though it were some precious object and looks at the two windows.

"What d'you pay for this ground floor of yours?"

"I've told you already: seventeen hundred."

"And you've got the lift too! Topping sunshine, might think you were in Nice! But that's not what I've come about: we've got an evening engagement."

"When?"

"When? Why, tonight."

"Oh!"

"Why 'Oh'? Is it awkward for you?"

"No. Do we take our act?"

"No, not the act, it's too important for that. Your dances. And I shall do my *Neurotic Pierrot* for them."

I jump up, really scared.

"My dances! But I can't! And besides, I lost my music at Aix! And then the girl who accompanies me has changed her address. If we'd at least had two days' notice. . . ."

"Out of the question," says Brague, unmoved. "They had Badet on the programme and she's ill."

"So that's it, a fill-in! If that isn't the limit! Do your *Pierrot* if you like, I'm not going to dance!"

Brague lights a cigarette and lets fall these two words: "Five hundred."

"For the two of us?"

"For you. And the same for me."

Five hundred! A quarter of my rent. Brague goes on smoking without looking at me: he knows I shall accept.

"Well of course, five hundred. What time do they want us?"

"Midnight, of course. You'll get busy about your music and everything, won't you? So long then, till this evening. Oh, by the way, Jadin's come back!"

He was closing the door, but I pull it open again: "She hasn't! When?"

"Yesterday, at midnight, you'd just gone. She looked awful! You'll see her; she's singing at our dump again. . . . Seventeen hundred, did you say? It's amazing. And women on every floor!"

And off he goes, grave and ribald.

An evening reception. . . . A social engagement. Those three words are quite enough to demoralise me. I don't dare say so to Brague, but I admit it to myself as I look at my funereal face in the glass, while a little shiver of cowardice grips the skin of my back.

To see *them* again . . . them whom I left so abruptly, those who once upon a time called me "Madame Renée", because it was their affectation never to give me my husband's name. Those men—and the women! The women who betrayed me with my husband, and the men who knew I was betrayed.

The time is past now when I used to see in every woman one of Adolphe's mistresses, actual or probable, and to such an adoring wife as I was, men were never much of a menace. But I have retained an idiotic and superstitious terror of those drawing-rooms where I might meet witnesses of accomplices of my past unhappiness.

This social engagement begins by spoiling my tête-à-tête lunch with my faithful old friend Hamond, a painter already old-fashioned and in poor health, who comes from time to time to eat his boiled macaroni with me. We don't talk much. He leans his head, like that of a sick Don Quixote, against the back of an armchair, and after lunch we play at making each other miserable. He talks to me about Adolphe Taillandy, not to hurt me, but to recall a time when he himself was happy. And I discuss with him his cruel young wife whom he foolishly married, and who went off four months later with I don't know whom.

These afternoons of melancholy in which we indulge leave us worn out, with faces so aged and bitter, and mouths so dry from having said all over again so many distressing things, that we swear never to do it again. But the next Saturday finds us reunited at my table, glad to see each other again and quite impenitent: Hamond has discovered an unknown anecdote about Adolphe Taillandy and, in order to enjoy the sight of my best friend sniffing back his tears, I have dug out of a drawer an amateur snapshot in which I am holding the arm of a little, fair-haired aggressive Madame Hamond, as upright as a serpent on its tail.

But this morning our lunch isn't going well. Although Hamond, numb with cold but gay, has brought me some beautiful December grapes, blue as plums, every grape a little skinful of sweet, tasteless water—this accursed evening engagement casts its shadow over my whole day.

At a quarter to twelve Brague and I arrive in the Avenue du Bois. It's a splendid house, they must be most sumptuously bored in it. The imposing footman who leads us to the "sitting-room reserved for the artistes" offers to help me off with my fur coat. I refuse tartly: does he suppose I am going to await the good pleasure of these ladies and gentlemen, dressed in four blue necklaces, a winged scarab and a few yards of gauze?

Much better brought up than I, the imposing footman does not insist and leaves us alone. Brague, looking so thin as to be almost insubstantial in his loose Pierrot's smock, under his white mask, stands stretching in front of a looking-glass. He likes this social engagement no better than I do. Not that he misses the "barrier of light" between himself and *them* as much as I do, but he has a poor opinion of what he calls drawing-room "clients", and treats the fashionable audience with something of the malicious indifference which he shows us.

"D'you suppose it's ever entered these people's heads to try to write my name properly?" says he, holding out a little card to me. "They call me Brag*n*e on their programmes!"

Very much hurt, at heart, he disappears, pursing up his thin, blood-red mouth, behind a door-curtain of greenery, for another imposing footman has that moment courteously called him by his mangled name.

In a quarter of an hour it will be my turn. I look at myself in the mirror and find myself ugly, deprived of the harsh electric-light which, in my dressing-room, floods the white walls, bathes the mirrors, penetrates one's make-up and gives it a velvety look. Will there be a carpet on the platform? If they could have risen, as Brague puts it, to a small row of footlights. This Salome wig grips my temples and makes my headache worse. I feel cold.

"Your turn, old girl! Go and do your stuff for them!"

Back again, Brague has already sponged his white face streaked with lines of sweat, and put on his coat while he is speaking.

"They're obviously people of standing. They don't make too much row. They talk, of course, but they don't laugh too loud. By the way, here's the two francs fifteen for my share of the taxi. I'm off."

"Aren't you going to wait for me?"

"What's the point? You go to Les Ternes and I to Montmartre, it's not the same way. Besides, I've got to give a lesson at nine tomorrow. So long, till tomorrow."

Now is the moment for my turn. My misshapen little pianist is already seated. With a hand trembling with stage-fright, I wrap round myself the veil which constitutes almost my whole costume, a circular veil of blue and violet measuring fifteen yards round.

At first I cannot distinguish anything through the fine mesh of my gauze cage. My bare feet are aware that they are treading on the short, firm pile of a fine Persian carpet. There are, alas, no footlights.

The bluish chrysalis which I represent awakens at the sound of a short prelude, and begins to writhe as my limbs slowly loosen. Little by little, the veil unwinds, fills, billows out and falls, revealing me to the eyes of the beholders, who have stopped their frantic chatter to gaze at me.

I see them. In spite of myself I see them. As I dance and crawl and turn, I see them, and I recognise them!

In the first row is a woman, still young, who was for quite a long time the mistress of my ex-husband. She was not expecting to see me this evening, and I was not thinking of her. Her sorrowful blue eyes, her one beauty, express as much fear as amazement. It is not me she fears; but my sudden presence has confronted her, brutally, with her own memories, she who suffered for Adolphe, she who was ready to leave everything for him, and wanted, with loud cries and noisy, imprudent tears, to kill her husband, and me too, and flee with Adolphe. By then he had already ceased to love her, and found her heavy on his hands. He used to confide her to my care for whole days together, charging me—what am I saying, ordering me—not to bring her back till seven o'clock; and never were there more harrowing tête-à-têtes than those of those two betrayed women who hated each other. Sometimes the poor creature, at the end of her tether, would burst into humiliated tears, and I would watch her weep, without pity for her tears, proud of controlling my own.

There she is, in the front row. They have used every inch of space and her chair is so close to the platform that I could bestow an ironical caress on her hair, which she dyes blonde because it is growing grey. She has aged in the past four years, and she looks at me with terror. She is looking through me at her sin, her despair, and her love which has perhaps ended by dying.

Behind her I recognise another woman too . . . and then one more. They used to come and have tea every week at my house in the days when I was married. Perhaps they slept with my husband; it does not matter if they did. None of them gives any sign of knowing me, but something reveals that they have recognised me, since one of them pretends to let her attention wander and talks very animatedly in a low voice to her neighbour, another exaggerates her short-sightedness, and a third, busy fanning herself and shaking her head, keeps whispering: "How hot it is, how terribly hot!"

They have changed their hair styles since the year when I abandoned all these false friends. Every one of them now conforms to the mode of swathing the hair round over the ears like a cap, binding it with a wide bandeau of ribbon or metal, which makes them look as though they were convalescent and not very clean. One no longer sees tempting napes of necks, or temples haloed in curls; one sees nothing but little muzzles— jaws, chins, mouths and noses—to which this year's fashion undeniably gives a markedly bestial appearance.

Round the sides and at the back there is a dark row of men, standing. Packed closely together they crane forward with that curiosity, that cynical courtesy which men of the world display towards a woman who is considered "déclassée", the woman whose finger-tips one used to kiss in her drawing-room and who now dances, half-naked, on a platform.

Come now, this won't do, I'm too clear-sighted this evening, and if I don't pull myself together my dancing will suffer for it. I dance and dance. A beautiful serpent coils itself along the Persian carpet, an Egyptian amphora tilts forward, pouring forth a cascade of perfumed hair, a blue and stormy cloud rises and floats away, a feline beast springs forwards, then recoils, a sphinx, the colour of pale sand, reclines at full length, propped on its elbows with hollowed back and straining breasts. I have recovered myself and forget nothing. Do these people really exist, I ask myself? No, they don't. The only real things are dancing, light, freedom and music. Nothing is real except making rhythm of one's thought and translating it into beautiful gestures. Is not the mere swaying of my back, free from any constraint, an insult to those bodies cramped by their long corsets, and enfeebled by a fashion which insists that they should be thin?

But there is something more worth while than humiliating them; I want, for one moment only, to charm them! It needs only a little more effort: already their heads, under the weight of their jewels and their hair, sway vaguely as they obediently follow my movements. At any moment now the vindictive light in all those eyes will go out, and the charmed creatures will all give in and smile at the same time.

The end of the dance, and the noise of the very controlled applause, break the spell. I disappear, to return and bow with a smile all round the room. At the back of the room a man's silhouette gesticulates and calls out "Bravo!" I know that voice and that tall black figure.

Why, it's my imbecile of the other evening! It's the Big-Noodle! Any doubts I may have about it are soon dispelled when I see him enter, with bent head, the little room where my pianist rejoins me. He is not alone, he is accompanied by another tall black noodle, who has the air of being the master of the house.

"Madame . . ." says he, bowing.

"Monsieur . . ."

"Will you permit me to thank you for having been so kind as to take part, on the spur of the moment, in . . . and to express to you all the admiration . . ."

"Really, Monsieur . . ."

"I am Henri Dufferein-Chautel."

"Ah, of course."

"And this is my brother, Maxime Dufferein-Chautel, who is extremely anxious to be presented to you."

My Big-Noodle of yesterday bows once more and manages to seize and kiss a hand which was busy gathering up the blue veil. Then he remains standing and saying nothing, much less at his ease than in my dressing-room.

Meanwhile Dufferein-Chautel No. 1 is awkwardly crumpling a closed envelope:

"I . . . I'm not sure whether it is to Monsieur Salomon, your impresario, or to you yourself that I should hand . . ."

Dufferein-Chautel No. 2, suddenly crimson under his brown skin, casts a furious, hurt glance at him, and there they both stand, each as foolish-looking as the other!

What is there embarrassing about all that? I cheerfully put them out of their misery: "Why, to me myself, Monsieur, it's quite simple! Give me that envelope, or rather slip it in with my music—for I will confess to you in confidence that my dancer's costume has no pockets!"

They both burst into relieved and slightly naughty laughter whereupon, declining the sly offer of Dufferein-Chautel No. 2, who fears on my behalf the toughs of Les Ternes, I am at last free to go home alone, joyfully clasping the five hundred francs that are my share, and to go to bed and sleep.

s i x

THIS FRIDAY EVENING, IN ORDER TO SLIP MY HAND INTO THE box where they put the letters—a little case nailed to the side of the box-office—I have to disturb a fine "pimp" in a cap, one of those classic types that abound in this district.

Even though his costume has been popularised in pictures and caricatures, in the theatre and the *café-concert*, the "bully" remains faithful to his sweater or his coloured, collarless shirt, to his cap and the jacket which he strains flatteringly tight round his hips by plunging his hands in the pockets, to his fag-end and his noiseless slippers.

On Saturdays and Sundays these gentlemen fill half our *Empyrée-Clichy*, outlining the gallery and stumping up two francs twenty-five to reserve in advance the cane-bottomed seats that practically touch the stage. They are the faithful, the devotees, who exchange remarks with the artistes, hiss or applaud them, and have a gift for interjecting the ribald criticism, the lewd exclamation that set the whole house in a roar.

Sometimes their success goes to their heads and then the whole thing becomes a riot. From one gallery to another they exchange pre-arranged remarks in spicy slang, followed by cat-calls and missiles which in turn lead to the prompt arrival of the police. It is as well for the artist on the stage to await the end of the storm with an expressionless face and a modest bearing, if he does not want to see the oranges, the programmes rolled into a ball, and the small coins change their direction. Simple prudence also cautions him not to go on with his interrupted song.

But these, I repeat, are brief storms, skirmishes reserved for Saturdays and Sundays. Order is very well maintained at the *Empyrée-Clichy*, where one feels the hand of Mme la Directrice —the Boss!

Dark and lively, covered with jewels, the Boss presides this evening, as every evening, in the box-office. Her brilliant, darting eyes miss nothing, and the theatre cleaners, in the mornings, do not dare to forget the dust in the dark corners. At the moment of my arrival those terrible eyes are withering a genuine apache, a hefty fellow not to be spurned, who has come to reserve one of the best cane-bottomed seats, close to the stage, those in the front row whose occupants squat like toads, with their arms on the railing in front and their chins on their crossed hands.

The Boss is turning him away, without any fuss, but with the demeanour of a lion-tamer!

"Pick up your money and hop it!"

The stalwart swings his arms and rocks like a bear: "What for, Madame Barnet? What've I done?"

"You and your, 'What've I done?' D'you think I didn't see you last Saturday? It was you in seat No. 1 in the gallery, wasn't it?"

"As if I could remember!"

"It was you who stood up during the pantomime, wasn't it, shouting out: 'She's only showing one tit, I want to see the two of 'em! I've paid two francs, one for each tit!' "

The stalwart turns crimson and protests, with his hand on his heart: "Me? Me? Now look here, Madame Barnet, I know how to behave, I know what's not done! Cross my heart, Madame Barnet, it wasn't me who . . ."

The queen of the *Empyrée* raises an inexorable right hand: "No fibs! I saw you, didn't I? So that's enough. There'll be no place for you for a week from today. Pick up your money and don't let me see you before Saturday or Sunday next. And now get out!"

The exit of the stalwart, barred for eight days, is well worth my losing a few minutes more. He goes off on his noiseless felt shoes, his back humped, and does not resume his insolent expression until he is on the pavement again. But his heart is not in it, his bearing is forced and, for a short while, there is no difference between this dangerous brute and a small boy deprived of his favourite pudding.

On the iron staircase, mingling with the air rising from the hot pipes, which smells of plaster, coal and ammonia, the voice of Jadin reaches me in snatches. The little wretch has found her familiar public again and got back her hold on them! You only have to hear, in the distance, the stormy laughter and the contented muttering with which they accompany and support her.

That warm harsh contralto, husky already from dissipation and perhaps the beginnings of consumption, finds its way to one's heart by the lowest and surest paths. If a "discriminating and artistic" producer were to stray in here and listen to Jadin singing, he would cry: "I'll take her and launch her, and in three months you'll see what I'll make of her!"

An arrogant and embittered failure, that is what he would make of her. Experiences of that kind are never encouraging; where could the ill-kempt Jadin shine better than here?

There she is on the staircase, just as she went away, would you believe it, with her over-long frock frayed out by her heels, and her Marie-Antoinette fichu, yellowed by the smoke of the auditorium, gaping open to show her gaunt, youthful thinness, her hunched shoulder, and her sulky mouth with its curled upper lip on whose down a moustache of powder lingers.

47

It gives me a keen and genuine pleasure to see that foul-mouthed child again, and she on her side rushes down the last steps to fall on me and squeeze my hands in her warm paws: for some unknown reason her "spree" has brought us closer together.

She follows me into my dressing-room where I risk a discreet reproach. "You know, Jadin, it was a rotten thing to do! You don't let people down like that!"

"I went to see my mother," says Jadin with great gravity.

But on catching sight of herself in the mirror in the act of lying, her whole childish face breaks into laughter and becomes one wide slit, like the faces of very young Persian cats.

"That's a good 'un, ain't it? . . . How bored you must all have been here without me!"

She radiates confident pride, surprised at heart that the *Empyrée-Clichy* had not put up its shutters during her absence.

"Haven't changed, have I? . . . Oh what lovely flowers! 'Scuse me."

With the swift gesture of a pickpocket, skilled from childhood at stealing oranges from the stalls, she seizes a huge purple rose before I have even opened the little envelope fastened to the side of a great sheaf of flowers which is standing waiting for me on the little make-up shelf.

MAXIME DUFFEREIN-CHAUTEL
With his respectful compliments

Dufferein-Chautel! At last I have found again the name of the Big-Noodle! Ever since the other evening, too lazy to open a *Tout-Paris*, I have called him successively Thureau-Dangin, Dujardin-Beaumetz, or Duguay-Trouin!

"Those are flowers all right, I'll say!" says Jadin while I undress. "They from your friend?"

I protest, with useless sincerity: "Dear me, no! Just someone thanking me . . . for an evening performance. . . ."

"That's a pity!" declares Jadin, as one who knows all about these things. "Only a gentleman gives flowers like that. The chap I ran off with the other day gave me just that kind."

The Vagabond

I burst out laughing: Jadin airing her views on the quality of flowers and "chaps" is irresistible. She turns quite red under her flour-powder and takes offence:

"What is it? P'raps you don't believe he was a gentleman? All right then, ask Canut, the stage-setter, to let you see what I brought back in the way of brass, last night when you'd just gone!"

"How much?"

"Sixteen hundred francs, dearie! Canut saw them, it isn't a yarn!"

Do I look sufficiently impressed? I fear not.

"And what are you going to do with it, Jadin?"

She plucks unconcernedly at the threads hanging from her old blue and white dress: "Don't suppose there'll be any for savings. I stood the stage hands a round of drinks. And then I lent—as she calls it—fifty francs to Myriame to pay for her coat. And the girls keep asking one after the other and saying they haven't got a bean. I really don't know! I say, there's Bouty! Hullo, Bouty!"

"Hullo, reveller!"

Bouty, having politely assured himself that my deshabille is covered by a kimono, pushes open the door of my dressing-room and shakes the hand that Jadin holds out, repeating "Hullo!" in a tender voice but with a rough gesture. But Jadin immediately forgets him and continues her conversation, standing behind me, and addressing herself to my image in the glass: "You know it makes me feel quite sick to have *as much money as that!*"

"But . . . won't you buy yourself some frocks . . . at least one . . . to replace this one?"

49

With the back of her hand she thrusts aside the straggling locks of her thin, straight hair: "What an idea! This dress'll do very well till the *Revue* comes on. Whatever would *they* say, if they saw I'd gone off up town to pick up enough brass to bring back a swell new outfit!"

She is right. *They* means her famous local public, exigent

and jealous, whom she has slightly betrayed but who forgive her on condition that she reappears before them badly turned out, badly shod, got up like an old rag-bag, but just the same as before her escapade, before her lapse.

After a pause Jadin goes on, quite at ease before the embarrassed silence of Bouty: "You see I bought myself what I needed most: a hat and a muff, as well as a scarf. And what a hat! You'll see it soon. . . . So long. You staying, Bouty? You know, Bouty, I'm rich, I'll stand you anything you like!"

"Not my line, thanks."

I've never seen Bouty so cold and disapproving. If I were to say aloud that he loves Jadin I should cover myself with ridicule; so I must be content to think it.

The little comedian departs soon after and I am left alone with my sheaf of roses, a large commonplace sheaf tied with pale green ribbon, just the sheaf one would expect from a "big noodle" such as my new admirer.

"With his respectful compliments. . . ." During the past three years I have received a good many compliments, if I may say so, but there was nothing respectful about them. And my old middle-class respectability, always vigilant, is secretly gratified, just as if those compliments—however veiled with respect they hope they are—were not asking for the same thing, always the same thing.

My short-sightedness does not prevent me from seeing, in the front row of the stalls, M. Dufferein-Chautel, junior, stiff and grave, with his black hair shining like the silk of a top-hat. Happy because he has seen from my look that I have recognised him, he follows my movements, my comings and goings on the stage, with his head, just as my dog Fossette does when I am dressing to go out.

seven

THE DAYS PASS. THERE IS NOTHING NEW IN MY LIFE, EXCEPT a patient man lying in wait for me.

We have just got over Christmas and the first of January. The Christmas evening performance was a hectic affair which shook the whole "dump" to its foundations. The public, more than half drunk, yelled like one man; the bespangled stage-boxes hurled mandarines and twopenny cigars at the upper galleries; Jadin, tipsy from lunch time on, lost the thread of her song and danced a frightful cancan on the stage, pulling up her skirts over her laddered stockings, a great lock of hair flapping down her back. A gala evening with our Boss presiding in her box, totting up the princely takings, with one eye on the sticky glasses cluttering the little shelves nailed to the backs of the stalls.

Brague also had been tipsy since dinner and was bubbling over with lewd fantasies like a little black goat. Alone in his dressing-room he improvised an extraordinary monologue of a moonstruck person defending himself against spectres, with cries of "Oh no, stop, let me alone!" or "Not that! Not that! Well, just once then . . ." and sighs and protests as of a man tortured by diabolical voluptuousness.

As for Bouty, writhing with the cramp his enteritis gave him, he sat sipping his bluish milk.

By way of a New Year's Eve celebration, I ate the beautiful hot-house grapes which my old friend Hamond had brought me, all alone with Fossette, who was crunching sweets sent by the Big-Noodle. But it needed a great deal of self-mockery not to fall a prey to the hurt jealousy of a child whom they have forgotten to ask to the party.

What in fact would I have liked? To have supper with Brague, or with Hamond, or with Dufferein-Chautel? Heavens, no! Well then, what? I am neither better nor worse than the rest of the world, and there are times when I should like to forbid others to enjoy themselves when I am bored.

It is a fact worth remarking that all my friends, the real, true ones like Hamond, are people who never have any luck and are incurably sad. Is it the "solidarity of ill-fortune" which binds us together? I don't think so. It seems to me rather that I attract and keep the friendship of those melancholy, solitary persons who are pledged to loneliness or the wandering life, as I am. Birds of a feather . . .

I brood on these cheerful ideas on my way back from visiting Margot. Margot is the younger sister of my ex-husband. Ever since childhood she has lugubriously borne this playful pet name which suits her about as well as a ring in the nose. She lives alone and, with her bobbed hair turning grey, her shirt blouse adorned with Russian embroidery, and her long black jacket, she looks rather like a Rosa Bonheur, turned Nihilist.

Fleeced by her husband, sponged on by her brother, robbed by her lawyer and cheated by her servants, Margot has taken refuge in a grim serenity made up of incurable kindness of heart and silent contempt. Everyone around her is so used to exploiting her that they continue to eat into her income and she lets it happen, merely giving way sometimes to sudden rages and dismissing her cook for a too-flagrant overcharge of a penny.

"I don't mind being robbed," she says, "but I do think they should take care how they do it." After which she relapses for days on end into her all-embracing contempt.

During my married life I knew Margot very little. Kind

though she was, she was always cold and far from talkative, and this reserve of hers did not encourage me to confide in her. But on the day when my break with Adolphe seemed final, she politely and briefly closed the door to my astonished husband and never saw him again. It was then I learnt that I had in Margot an ally, a friend and a support, since it is from her that I get the fifteen louis a month which keep me from destitution. "Go on, take it!" said Margot. "You won't be doing me any harm. It's only the ten francs a day that Adolphe has always touched me for!"

It is true that I should never turn to Margot for consolation or for that tonic cheerfulness that they tell me will be good for me. But at least Margot loves me in her own way, her discouraged and discouraging way, though prophesying that I shall come to a wretched end.

"As for you, my girl," she said to me once again today, "you'll be lucky if you don't get caught up all over again with a man just like Adolphe. Like me, you're made to be imposed on. But it's a waste of my time talking to you. Burnt child though you are, you'll go back to the fire, you mark my words! You're so obviously one of those who need more than one Adolphe to teach them."

"Really, Margot, you're extraordinary! Every time I see you, you take me to task like this," I reproached her, laughingly. " 'You're this, you're that, you're one of those who, one of those that . . .' Do at least wait until I've sinned, it'll be time enough to blame me for it afterwards."

Margot put on one of those expressions that make her look very tall, so lofty do they seem.

"I'm not blaming you, my girl. And I shan't blame you any more when you have sinned, as you put it. Only, it will be very difficult for you to refrain from committing *the* folly, for there is only one: the folly of beginning all over again. I know what I'm talking about. Even though," she added with a strange smile, "*I* never had any senses!"

"Well then, Margot, what ought I to do? What do you feel

53

is wrong with my present life? Do you think I ought to shut myself up, as you do, for fear of a worse ill, and like you love nothing but little short-haired Brabançon terriers?"

"Take jolly good care you don't!" burst out Margot, with a sudden childlike gaiety. "Little Brabançon terriers indeed! They're the nastiest brutes possible. Look at that creature," she went on, pointing to a little tawny bitch who looked like a shorn squirrel. "I sat up with her for fifteen nights when she had bronchitis. Yet if I happen to leave her alone for an hour in the house, the little horror pretends not to recognise me and growls at my heels as if I were a tramp. . . . But apart from all those things, are you well, my child?"

"Very well, thank you, Margot."

"Tongue? Whites of the eyes? Pulse?"

She turns back my eyelids and presses my wrist with an assured, professional hand, exactly as if I were a little Brabançon. For Margot and I both know the value of health, and the misery of losing it. One manages to live alone and one gets used to it; but to languish alone in fever, to cough through an interminable night, to stagger on tottering legs to a window whose panes are lashed with rain, and then to return to a rumpled, sagging bed—alone, alone, alone!

For a few days last year I knew the horror of lying, vaguely delirious, and dreading, in my half-lucidity, that I might die slowly, far from everyone and forgotten. Ever since then, following Margot's example, I take good care of myself and look after my insides, my throat, my stomach and my skin, with the slightly fanatical strictness of a proprietor who is devoted to his possessions.

54

I have been thinking today of that odd remark of Margot's, that she for her part "never had any senses". And what about me and my senses? Now I come to think of it, it's a very long time since I thought of them.

Margot appears to think that the whole "question of the senses" is important. If I am to believe literature—the best and the worst too—no voice can compete with the voice of the senses. What is one to believe?

Brague once said to me, in the tone of one giving medical advice: "You know, it's not healthy to live as you do." And, like Margot, he added: "Anyway, you'll come to it, like all the others. Remember what I'm telling you."

I don't like thinking of that. Brague is always ready to lay down the law and play at being infallible. It doesn't mean a thing. All the same I don't like thinking of it.

At the music-hall I join, without the slightest affectation of prudery, in conversations where they discuss "the question of the senses" with statistical and surgical precision, and I take the same detached and respectful interest in them as I do in reading in a newspaper of the ravages of the plague in Asia. I am quite ready to be moved but I prefer to remain half incredulous. All the same I don't much like thinking of it.

And besides, there is that man—the Big-Noodle—who contrives to live in my shadow and tread in my footsteps with the obstinacy of a dog. I find flowers in my dressing-room and Fossette gets a little nickel trough for her meals; three minute animal mascots sit chatting nose to nose on my writing-table: an amethyst cat, a chalcedony elephant and a turquoise toad. A circlet of jade, green as a tree-frog, bound the stalks of a bunch of greenish lilies which was handed to me on New Year's Day. And in the street I too often run into that same Dufferein-Chautel, who bows with a look of surprise that would deceive no one.

He forces me to remember, too often, the existence of desire, that imperious demi-god, that unleashed faun who gambols round love and does not obey love; and to remember that I am alone, healthy, still young, and rejuvenated by my long, moral convalescence.

Senses? Yes, I have them . . . or I had them in the days when Adolphe Taillandy condescended to concern himself with them. Shy senses they were, normal senses, glad of the conventional caress which was enough for them, afraid of any refinements or erotic complications, slow to rouse but slow to quench, in short, healthy senses.

Betrayal and long-drawn-out grief have anaesthetised them . . . for how much longer, I wonder? On days when I am gay and light-hearted, the pleasure of feeling myself pure, and cut off from what made me a woman like any other, is enough to make me say to myself "For ever!" But there are also lucid days when I reason harshly with myself. "Take care! Be always on guard! Everyone who approaches you is suspect, but you are your own worst enemy. Don't proclaim that you are dead, empty, light: the beast whom you forget is hibernating, and fortifying himself with a long sleep."

And then I forget once again the memory of what I was, in the fear of becoming once more *alive*; I want nothing, I regret nothing . . . until the next time my confidence lands me in disaster, until that inevitable moment of crisis when, with terror in my eyes, I see advancing towards me, with gentle, powerful hands, the sadness that guides and accompanies one in all the pleasures of the flesh.

eight

FOR SEVERAL DAYS PAST BRAGUE AND I HAVE BEEN REHEARS-ing a new act. There will be a forest, a grotto, an old troglodyte, a young hamadryad, and a faun in the prime of life.

The faun is Brague, I am to be the woodland nymph, and as for the old troglodyte, we haven't yet thought about him. He only appears at intervals, and to play this part, Brague says: "There's a young ruffian of eighteen among my pupils who'll make a perfect prehistoric!"

They have kindly lent us the stage at the *Folies* from ten to eleven in the mornings for our rehearsals. Stripped of its backcloths, the whole of the deep, bare stage is visible. How sad and grey it all looks when I arrive, with no corset on, a sweater instead of a blouse, and black satin knickers under my short skirt.

I envy Brague for being, at no matter what hour, always himself, alert, swarthy and authoritative. I struggle feebly against the cold, and the sluggish, sickening atmosphere not yet rid of the stale smells of the night before and still smelling of humanity and sour punch. The tinny old rehearsal piano grinds out the new music, my hands grip each other and part with difficulty, my gestures are constricted, close to my body, I hunch my shoulders with the cold and feel myself mediocre, awkward, lost.

Brague, used to my morning inertia, has also learnt the secret of how to cure it. He badgers me without respite, running round me like a terrier, showering brief encouragements and sharp exclamations which make me tingle as though I had been lashed.

A cloud of dust rises from the auditorium: it is the hour when the cleaners are brushing away the mud that has dried on the carpets, together with all the rubbish dropped the evening before: papers, cherry-stones, cigarette-ends, and dried dung from the soles of shoes.

Towards the back of the stage—for we are only lent a section of it, a strip about two yards wide—a troupe of acrobats are at work on their thick carpet: they are handsome, fair-haired, rosy Germans, silent and intent on the job. Their working tights are dirty, and by way of relaxation and pastime during the intervals of their act, they keep on exercising; two of them, laughing sleepily, attempt a miracle of unattainable equilibrium . . . which they will perhaps achieve next month. When the rehearsal is over, they concentrate very seriously on the perilous education of the youngest of the troupe, an urchin with the face of a little girl, beneath long fair curls, whom they throw in the air and catch on a foot or a hand, an airy little creature who seems to fly, with his locks streaming out horizontally behind him or standing on end like a flame above his head while he falls back to earth, feet together and pointing downwards and arms glued to his body.

"As you were!" cries Brague. "You've bungled that movement again! Of all the lackadaisical rehearsals! Can't you possibly attend to what you're doing?"

It's difficult, I must admit. Overhead now there are some gymnasts swinging on three trapezes, and exchanging shrill cries like the cries of swallows. The glittering nickel of the metal trapezes, the squeak of rosined hands on the polished bars, all that expenditure of elegant and supple strength going on around me, that methodical contempt of danger, finally exalt and fire me with the desire to emulate them. And that is the moment when they turn us out, just when I was beginning to be conscious of the beauty of a perfected gesture, the right-ness of an expression of horror or desire, suddenly adorning my body like a rich ornament.

Roused thus too late, I use up the rest of my energy in returning on foot with Fossette, whom rehearsals fill with a silent rage which she works off outside on dogs bigger than herself. Like a brilliant mime, she terrorises them with a single twitch of her Japanese dragon-mask, a hideous grimace which makes her black eyes start out of her head, and curls back her lips to reveal, beneath their pink undersides, a few white teeth set askew like palings of a fence blown in all directions by the wind.

As a result of having grown up in the profession, Fossette knows the music-hall better than I do; she trots about in dark basements, bowls along corridors, and finds her way by the familiar smell of soapy water, rice powder and ammonia. Her brindled body is used to being clasped in arms coated with pearl white; she condescends to eat the sugar that the supers scrounge from the saucers in the café downstairs. A creature of whims, sometimes she insists that I should take her with me in the evenings, and on other days, coiled round like a turban in her basket, she watches me go with the contempt of a dowager who, for her part, likes to digest her meal slowly.

"It's Saturday, Fossette, we must hurry! Hamond will have arrived before us!"

Instead of taking a cab, we have run like two mad creatures, because the air, this morning, is full of that soft and surprising sweetness that comes before the spring. We catch up with Hamond just as he reaches my white box of a house, the col-our of sculptured butter.

But Hamond is not alone: he is talking on the pavement with . . . with Dufferein-Chautel, junior, christened Max-ime, and *known* as the Big-Noodle.

"What! You again!"

Without giving him time to protest, I questioned Hamond severely. "You know M. Dufferein-Chautel?"

"Certainly I do," says Hamond calmly. "So do you, I see. But I knew him when he was quite small. I still have in a drawer a photograph of a boy with a white armband: 'In memory of the First Communion of Maxime Dufferein-Chautel, May 15th 18 . . .'"

"So you have!" cries the Big-Noodle. "Mother sent it you because she thought I looked so beautiful."

I don't join in their laughter. I am not pleased that they know each other. And I feel uncomfortable under the strong, noonday light, with my hair out of curl under my fur cap, my nose shiny for lack of powder, and my mouth dry with hunger and thirst.

I hide my shapeless, laced rehearsal boots under my skirt. The kid is so rubbed now that it shows the blue, but they grip my ankles well and their worn soles are as supple as those of dancing slippers. Especially as the Big-Noodle is looking me over as if he had never seen me before.

I stifle a sudden childish longing to cry and instead I ask him, as if I were about to bite him: "What is it? Have I got a smut on my nose?"

He takes his time to reply: "No . . . but . . . it's odd . . . when one has only seen you in the evening one would never believe you have grey eyes. They look brown on the stage."

"Yes, I know. I've been told so before. You know, Hamond, the omelette will be cold. Goodbye, Monsieur."

Come to that, I too had never seen him so well, in full daylight. His deep-set eyes are not black, as I thought, but a rather tawny brown, like the eyes of sheep-dogs.

I thought they would never stop shaking hands! And that little tart, Fossette, saying "goodbye to the gentleman", and grinning like an ogress from ear to ear! And the Big-Noodle putting on the look of a beggar at the pastry-cook's window, just because I spoke of an omelette! If he thinks I'm going to invite him!

Quite unfairly, I lay the blame for all of it on Hamond. So I remain silent as I hurriedly give my face and hands a brief wash before rejoining my old friend in the little study where Blandine is laying the table. For I have suppressed once and for all that sad and useless room known as a dining-room and used for only one hour in the twenty-four. But I must admit that Blandine sleeps in, and that an extra room would have cost me too much.

"Well, well, so you know Maxime!" cries Hamond as he unfolds his napkin.

I was expecting that!

"I? I don't know him at all! I had an evening engagement at his brother's house, where I met him. That's all."

I forbear—why, I wonder?—to mention the first interview, when the Big-Noodle, in a state of excitement, burst into my dressing-room.

"Well, he knows you. And he admires you a great deal. In fact I rather think he is in love with you."

Subtle Hamond! I look at him with that sly, feline mirth that masculine naïvety inspires in us.

"He knows you like roses, and sweets flavoured with pistachio. He's ordered a collar for Fossette . . ."

I spring to my feet: "He's ordered a collar for Fossette! . . . Oh well, after all that's nothing to do with me!" I say, laughing. "Fossette's a creature with no morals: she'll accept, she's quite capable of it!"

"We spoke of you, naturally. I thought you were very good friends."

"Oh Hamond, I would have told you!"

His friendly jealously flattered, my old friend lowers his eyes.

"He's a very nice chap, I assure you."

"Who is?"

"Maxime. I met his mother, who is a widow, in . . . let's see now, it must be thirty . . . no, thirty-five. . . ."

Off he goes, and I have to endure the history of the Duffer-ein-Chautels, mother and son. A managing woman, she runs the whole estate, saw mills in the Ardennes, acres of forest land. Maxime, rather lazy, is the youngest and most spoilt of her sons, much more intelligent than he seems, thirty-three and a half years old. . . .

"Fancy! Just like me!"

Hamond leans towards me, over the little table, with the attention of a miniaturist: "Are you thirty-three, Renée?"

"Alas!"

"Don't say it. No one would know."

"Oh, I know very well that on the stage . . ."

"Nor in everyday life either."

That is as far as his compliment gets and Hamond goes on with the history of the Dufferein-Chautels. Displeased, I suck some grapes. The Big-Noodle is insinuating himself into my life more than I have allowed him. At this hour Hamond and I ought, as our custom is, to be stirring up those bad old memories that blossom weekly in the bitter aroma of our steaming cups.

Poor Hamond! It is for my sake that he is departing from his beloved, gloomy habit. I well know that my solitude makes him anxious; if he dared he would say to me, like a paternal go-between:

"There is the lover you need, my dear! Good health, doesn't gamble, doesn't drink, well-enough off. . . . You'll thank me!"

n i n e

FOUR DAYS MORE AND I LEAVE THE *EMPYRÉE-CLICHY!* EVERY time I come to the end of a rather long engagement at a *café-concert*, I have the odd impression, during the last days, of being given a freedom I have not desired. Happy though I am to be free and able to spend my evenings at home, I am not in a hurry to enjoy it, and when I stretch and say "At last!" there is a lack of spontaneity about it.

All the same this time I really believe I am glad, and as I sit in Brague's dressing-room I give him a list, at which he mocks, of the urgent tasks which are going to fill my holidays.

"I'm having all the divan cushions re-covered, you know. And then I'm pushing the divan itself right into the corner, and I'm going to have an electric lamp fixed above it."

"Splendid! It'll look just like a brothel," says Brague gravely.

"Silly ass! And besides that, oh well, I've heaps of things to do. It's such ages since I paid any attention to my home."

"It certainly is!" agrees Brague, drily. "And who are you doing all this for?"

"What d'you mean, who for? For myself, of course!"

Brague turns from the mirror a moment, showing a face in which the right eye, the only one he has rubbed with blue, looks as if it were ringed with terrific bruises.

"For yourself? Just for yourself? You'll forgive me but I find that a bit . . . fatuous. Besides, d'you suppose I'm going to let *The Pursuit* lie dormant? You'd better be ready to be off at a

63

moment's notice for one of those first-rate establishments in the provinces and abroad. And by the way, Salomon, the agent, asked me to tell you to drop round and see him."

"Oh! already?"

Brague shrugs his shoulders and says, sharply: "There you go as usual, with your 'Oh! already?' Yet if I were to tell you there was nothing doing, you'd keep on like a mosquito: 'When do we start? When do we start?' You're all exactly alike, you womenfolk."

"My view too," agrees the melancholy voice of Bouty, behind us.

He has grown thinner than ever this past month, has Bouty, and he "tires" more and more. I steal a glance at him when he is not looking, so as not to hurt him; but what can one make out under that red mask with the white-rimmed eyes? Silently we listen to the voice of Jadin above us:

> "My sweet little Mignonet-te
> I pray you may never regret
>   The wonderful day
>   When I gave you a spray,
> A spray—of mignonette!"

The composer of the *Waltz of the Mignonette*, an experienced man who knows his job, has cunningly contrived a suggestive pause in the middle of the last line of the chorus.

"So in four days more you'll be making tracks?" asks the little funny-man abruptly, raising his head.

"Yes, in four days. I've enjoyed being here. It's so peaceful."

"So peaceful!" protests Bouty, sceptically. "I can think of places more peaceful than this. You'll easily find better. I'm not running down our public, but all the same they're a pretty low lot. Oh, I know one can keep up one's standard anywhere," he goes on, seeing me shrug as if I thought that unimportant. "But all the same . . . just listen to them bawling now! How d'you suppose a woman, a young woman I mean, with no proper notions, always up to larks and ready to go on the spree, can learn good behaviour in the middle of all that? When she's a scatterbrained, rackety girl, I mean . . . like Jadin, for instance?"

Poor little Bouty, it is your unhappy love that has suddenly given you these aristocratic ideas, this contempt for a public which applauds you; and in seeking and finding an excuse for Jadin, you spontaneously invent the theory of the influence of environment, in which I don't believe!

The Russian dancers have gone, and Antonieff—the "grand-duke"—and his dogs have gone too. Where? No one knows. None of us has had the curiosity to find out. Other turns have come to take their place, some engaged for seven days and others for four, since the *Revue* is now so imminent; on the stage and in the corridors I run into new faces with which, by way of a friendly and discreet greeting, I exchange a half-smile or a questioning look.

The only ones who remain from the former programme are ourselves, Jadin, who is to create—Heavens above!—various roles in the *Revue*, and Bouty. We chat in a melancholy way in the evenings, like veterans of the *Empyrée-Clichy* forgotten when the young regiment marched away.

Where shall I find again those whom I have known here? In Paris, Lyons, Vienna or Berlin? Perhaps never, perhaps no-where. We shall meet for five minutes in the office of Salomon, the agent, with noisy greetings and stagey handclasps, just long enough to know that we still exist and to utter the indispensable "What are you doing?" and to learn in reply that "things are going nicely" or that "things aren't shaping too well".

Things aren't shaping too well. . . . This is the vague circumlocution my wandering companions use to cover hard times, "restings", money troubles, and destitution. Puffed up and sustained by that heroic vanity which endears them to me, they never admit. A few of them, at the end of their tether, find a little part to fill in a *real* theatre, and oddly enough they never boast of this. Patient and obscure, they wait there for the renewal of luck which will bring them an engagement at a music-hall, the blessed hour which will see them in a spangled skirt again, or evening clothes smelling of benzine, once more facing the spotlight *in their repertoire!*

"No, things aren't shaping well," some will tell me, adding: "I'm trying the films again."

The motion picture, which threatened the humble *café-concert* artistes with ruin, is now their salvation. In it they adapt themselves to an anonymous labour which brings them no fame, which they do not like, which upsets their habits and changes the times of their meals, their leisure and their work. Hundreds live by it in times of unemployment, and many settle down in it. But if the films become glutted with supers and stars, what will they do?

"Things aren't shaping well . . . no, things aren't shaping well."

They utter the phrase in a casual but at the same time serious way, without overdoing it and without whining, swinging their hat or a pair of old gloves in their hands. They swagger, tightly buttoned in a full-skirted overcoat of the fashion of two seasons ago; for the essential, the indispensable thing, is not the possession of a clean suit but of a "really classy" overcoat which covers everything: threadbare waistcoat, shapeless jacket, trousers yellowed at the knees; a dashing, flashy overcoat, which makes an impression on the director or the agent, and which in the last resort enables one to throw off a "things aren't shaping well" in the jaunty tone of a man of means.

Where shall we be next month? In the evenings Bouty prowls aimlessly up and down the corridor of the dressing-rooms, and keeps up a gentle coughing until I half open my door to invite him to sit down for a moment in my room. He squeezes his flanks, like a lean dog's, into a rickety chair with its white paint flaking off, and tucks his feet under him so as not to interfere with my movements. Brague comes to join us and crouches like a gipsy, with his behind against the hot pipes. Standing between them, I finish dressing, and my red skirt, embroidered with yellow, fans them as I pass. Though we have no wish to talk, we chatter to overcome a brooding longing to be silent, to huddle against each other and grow sentimental.

Brague manages better than the rest of us to remain clear-sighted, interested and active; he is still commercially eager for the future. For me the future, whether it is here or there, is . . . My lately acquired and rather artificial liking for uproot-ings and travel fits in happily with the peaceful fatalism natural to the bourgeoise that I am. A gipsy henceforth I certainly am, and one whom tours have led from town to town, but an orderly gipsy, careful to mend her well-brushed garments her-self; a gipsy who nearly always carries her slender fortune on her person; but in the little suède bag, the coppers are in one compartment, the silver in another, while the gold is pre-ciously hidden in a secret pocket.

A vagabond, maybe, but one who is resigned to revolving on the same spot like my companions and brethren. It is true that departures sadden and exhilarate me, and whatever I pass through—new countries, skies pure or cloudy, seas under rain the colour of a grey pearl—something of myself catches on it and clings so passionately that I feel as though I were leaving behind me a thousand little phantoms in my image, rocked on the waves, cradled in the leaves, scattered among the clouds. But does not a last little phantom, more like me than any of the others, remain sitting in my chimney corner, lost in a dream and as good as gold as it bends over a book which it forgets to open?

Part Two

o n e

"WHAT A CHARMING, COSY NEST! I MUST SAY IT'S HARD TO imagine your existence in the music-hall when one sees you here between this rosy lamp and that vase of carnations."

Such was the parting remark of my admirer the first time he came to dinner at my flat, with Hamond the go-between. For I have an admirer. Only this old-fashioned name seems to suit him: he is neither my lover, nor my flame, nor my gigolo; he is my admirer.

"What a charming, cosy nest!" That evening I laughed bitterly behind his back. To think that a shaded lamp, a crystal vase filled with sparkling water, an easy chair drawn up close to the table, and a divan whose shabbiness is masked by a cunning disorder of cushions—to think that all that can so dazzle the casual visitor as to make him imagine, between these faded green walls, the secluded, contemplative and studious life of a gifted woman. Ah, but he hasn't noticed the dusty inkpot, the dry pen and the uncut book on the empty box of stationery!

An old spray of holly, contorted as though it had been through fire, curls over the edge of an earthenware pot. The cracked glass of a little pastel (one of Adolphe Taillandy's sketches) waits in vain to be replaced. Round the electric bulb which lights the fireplace I have carelessly pinned, and then forgotten, a torn sheet of paper. A pile of five hundred postcards—scenes from *The Pursuit*—, banded with grey paper, lies on a fifteenth-century carved ivory and threatens to crush it.

The whole place gives an impression of indifference, neglect, hopelessness, almost of imminent departure. Cosy? Could one so describe anything that happens in the evening here, under the lamp with its faded shade?

After my two guests had left I laughed, and sighed with weariness, and the night that followed was so troubled by an obscure sense of shame, born of the very admiration of the Big-Noodle, that it seemed endless. His belief in me, the innocent belief of a man very much in love, enlightened me about myself that evening just as an unexpected mirror, at a street corner or on a staircase, suddenly reveals blemishes and saggings in one's face and figure.

But since then there have been other evenings when Hamond came with my admirer, or my admirer without Hamond. My old friend conscientiously performs what he calls his sordid task. Sometimes he presides with the brilliant ease of a former wit over the visits of his pupil who, without him, I admit in all sincerity, would be too much for me. Sometimes he effaces himself, though not for long, or keeps us waiting, just long enough, exercising on my behalf that social diplomacy of his which was getting rusty.

I do not dress up for them, and change neither my pleated white blouse nor my plain dark skirt. I "let my face go" when they are there, mouth tired and shut and eyes deliberately dull, and to my admirer's persistence I oppose the passive bearing of a girl whom her parents want to marry against her will. The only thing I take trouble over, for my own sake more than theirs, is the sketchy, deceptive interior where I live so little; Blandine has condescended to explore the dusty corners of the study, and the cushions of the armchair in front of the table are still flattened from the last time I rested there.

I have an admirer. Why should it be this one and not another? I have no idea. I look in astonishment at this man who has managed to worm his way into my flat. My word, how desperately he wanted to! Luck was on his side every time, and Hamond helped him. One day, when I was all alone, I opened the door to a timid ring; and how could I possibly have thrust out this creature standing there awkwardly waiting, his arms full of roses, with Hamond beside him gazing imploringly at me? He has managed to worm his way in here, and no doubt it was bound to happen.

Every time he comes now, I have to get to know his face as though I had never seen it before. On each side of his nose there is a crease, already quite deep, which disappears under his moustache, and he has the rather swarthy red lips which you find in people who are almost too dark. His hair and his eyebrows and lashes are as black as the devil, and it needed a very bright ray of sunshine one day to show me that, beneath all that black, my admirer's eyes are a tawny brown, and very deep set.

Standing up, he really is a Big-Noodle, stiff, awkward and nothing but bones. Sitting, or half-reclining on the divan, he seems to grow supple all of a sudden, and to enjoy the pleasure of being quite a different man, lazy and relaxed, moving his hands gracefully as he settles his head indolently back against the cushions.

When I know that he cannot see me, I observe him, feeling vaguely shocked at the thought that I do not know him at all and that the presence of this young man in my flat is as unexpected as a piano in a kitchen.

How is it that he, who is in love with me, is not in the least disturbed that he knows me so little? He clearly never gives that a thought, and his one idea is first to reassure me and afterwards to conquer me. For if he has very quickly learnt— on Hamond's advice, I'll bet—to hide his desire and subdue his look and his voice when he speaks to me, if he pretends, cunning as an animal, to have forgotten that he wants to possess me, neither does he show any eagerness to find out what I am like, to question me or read my character, and I notice that he pays more attention to the play of light on my hair than to what I am saying.

How strange all that is! There he sits close to me, the same ray of sun gliding over his cheek and mine, and if it makes his nostrils glow ruby-red, it must be tinting mine bright coral. He is not there, he is a thousand leagues away! I keep wanting to get up and say to him: "Why are you here? Go away!" And I do nothing of the kind.

Does he think? Does he read? Does he work? I believe he belongs to that large rather commonplace class of persons who are interested in everything and do absolutely nothing. Not a trace of wit, a certain quickness of comprehension, a very adequate vocabulary enhanced by a beautiful rich voice, that readiness to laugh with a childish gaiety that one sees in many men—such is my admirer.

To be entirely honest, let me mention what I like best in him: a look that is sometimes absent and seeking, and that kind of private smile in the eyes which one sees in sensitive people who are both violent and shy.

He has travelled, but just like everyone else: not very far and not often. He has read what everyone reads, he knows "quite a few people" and cannot name three intimate friends, in addition to his elder brother. I forgive him all this ordinariness for the sake of a simplicity which has nothing humble about it, and because he finds nothing to say about himself.

His glance rarely meets mine, which I turn aside. I cannot forget the reason for his presence and for his patience. And yet what a difference between the man sitting there on this divan and the cruel animal, full of fierce desire, who forced the door of my dressing-room! Nothing about me shows that I remember our first meeting, except the fact that I hardly talk to the Big-Noodle. Whatever subject he tries, I answer him briefly, or else I address to Hamond the reply destined for my admirer. This type of indirect conversation gives our meetings a slowness and a false gaiety that are quite indescribable.

t w o

I AM STILL REHEARSING THE NEW ACT WITH BRAGUE. SOME-
times in the mornings the *Folies-Bergère* takes us in, or else
the *Empyrée-Clichy* lends us its stage for an hour; or else
we wander from the *Brasserie Gambrinus*, which is used to the
noise of Baret's tours, to the Cernuschi dancing-hall.

"It's beginning to look like something," says Brague, as eager for compliments for others as for himself.

The Old Troglodyte rehearses with us: he is a famished-
looking youth of eighteen, whom Brague assists, dumbfounds
and shatters with insults till I am moved to pity: "You're really
going too far, Brague, he's going to cry!"

"Just let him cry and I'll boot him in the backside! He's got
to work, not weep!"

Perhaps he is right. The Old Troglodyte gulps back his
tears, humps his back in what he hopes is a "prehistoric" way,
and sets himself to guarding a Hamadryad attitudinising in a
white knitted sweater.

One morning last week Brague took the trouble to come in
person to warn me that there would be no rehearsal the following day. He found Hamond, Dufferein-Chautel and myself
finishing lunch. I had to keep Brague a few minutes, offer him
coffee and introduce him to my guests. And I saw his bright
little black eyes linger furtively on my admirer with a curious
satisfaction, a sort of security, which made me feel stupidly
uncomfortable.

When I accompanied him to the door again my comrade did not question me or permit himself any familiar allusions, and my embarrassment was redoubled. It would have been too absurd to explain: "That's a friend of Hamond's who came to lunch. He's just a pal, you know."

Fossette is now wearing a collar of red morocco with gilded studs, in deplorable sporting taste. I have not dared to say that I found it ugly. Wretched little servile female that she is, she fawns on the well-dressed gentleman who smells of man and tobacco, and knows just the right way to pat her back.

Blandine outdoes herself, cleaning the windows and, without being asked, bringing in the tea-tray when my admirer is there.

All of them, following the example of my old friend Hamond, look as if they are plotting against me in favour of Maxime Dufferein-Chautel. Alas, it costs me so little effort to remain invulnerable! Invulnerable, and worse than insensitive: shrinking. For when I give my hand to my admirer, the touch of his long hand, warm and dry, surprises and displeases me. I cannot brush against the stuff of his jacket without a little nervous shudder, and when he speaks I involuntarily avoid his breath, healthy though it is. I could never bring myself to tie his tie, and I would rather drink from Hamond's glass than from his. Why?

It is because . . . this fellow is *a man*. In spite of myself I cannot forget that he is *a man*. Hamond is not a man, he is a friend. And Brague is a comrade; so is Bouty. The slender, muscular acrobats who reveal, beneath their shimmering tights, the most flattering details of their anatomy, well, they are just acrobats!

Has it ever occurred to me that Brague, who in *The Pursuit* clasps me hard enough to bruise my ribs, and looks as if he were crushing my mouth under a passionate kiss, had a sex? No. And yet the most fleeting glance from my admirer, the most correct handshake, remind me why he is there and what he hopes. What a delightful pastime he would be for a coquette! What an agreeable flame, provocative and determined!

The trouble is that I do not know how to flirt. I have neither the disposition, nor the experience, nor the light touch necessary, and above all—oh above all—I have the memory of my husband.

If for a single instant I call to mind Adolphe Taillandy when he was on the job, by which I mean working, with that ruthless unswerving pursuit characteristic of him, to seduce a woman or a young girl, I immediately grow frigid, shrinking, and utterly hostile to "the business of love". I see again, too well, his look of conquest, with lowered lids, sly, childish mouth, and that trick of dilating his nostrils when a particular perfume drifted by. Ugh! All that manoeuvring, those elaborate preparations for love, for a goal that one cannot even call love, am I to encourage and even to imitate that sort of thing? Poor Dufferein-Chautel! Sometimes it seems to me that it is you who are being deceived here, and that I ought to tell you . . . to tell you what? That I have become an old maid again with no temptations, and that the four walls of my dressing-room at the music-hall are for me a cloister?

No, I shall not tell you that because, like those who have got to the tenth lesson at the Berlitz School, we only know how to exchange elementary phrases where the words *bread, salt, window, temperature, theatre* and *family* play a great part.

You are a *man*, so much the worse for you! Everyone in my house seems to remember it, not in the way I do, but in order to congratulate you because of it, from Blandine who gazes at you with a never-wearying satisfaction, to Fossette whose wide doggy smile says just as clearly: "At last *a man* in the house— behold THE MAN!"

I don't know how to talk to you, poor Dufferein-Chautel. I hesitate between my own *personal* language, which is rather brusque, does not always condescend to finish its sentences, but sets great store on getting its technical terms exact—the language of a one-time blue-stocking—and the slovenly, lively idiom, coarse and picturesque, which one learns in the music-hall, sprinkled with expressions like: "You bet!" "Shut up!" "I'm clearing out!" "Not my line!"

Unable to decide, I choose silence.

three

"DEAR HAMOND, HOW HAPPY I AM TO BE LUNCHING WITH you! No rehearsal today, but sunshine, and you, it's all perfect!"

My old friend, who is suffering from stabs of rheumatism, smiles at me, flattered. He is at present very thin and looks older and somehow light. Being very tall, too, all that, and his bony, aquiline nose gives him a great resemblance to the Knight of the Dolorous Countenance.

"Yet I rather think we have already had the pleasure of lunching together this week? What overflowing affection for my old carcass, Renée!"

"That's just it, I *am* overflowing! It's a fine day, I feel gay, and . . . we're all alone!"

"Which means?"

"That the Big-Noodle isn't here, you've guessed it!"

Hamond shakes his long, melancholy head: "It's an aversion, there's no doubt of it!"

"Not at all, Hamond, not at all! It's . . . it's nothing. All right then, I'll tell you, I've been thinking of being frank with you for some days past: the trouble is I can't discover that I have the slightest feeling for Dufferein-Chautel, unless perhaps it is distrust."

"That's something."

"I haven't even any opinion about him."

"Well then it'll be a pleasure for me to offer you mine. The honest creature has no history."

"Not enough!"

"Not enough? You're really too difficult! You don't encourage him to tell you what he has."

"That would be the last straw! Can't you see him, with his large hand on his large heart: 'I am not a man like other men. . . .' That's what he'd say, isn't it? Men always say the same thing as women do, at such times."

Hamond's eyes dwell on me with an ironic look.

"I always like you, Renée, when you assume an experience which—happily—you lack. 'Men do this . . . men say that. . . .' Where did you glean such assurance? Men! Men! Have you known so many?"

"Only one. But what a one!"

"That's just it. But you aren't accusing Maxime of reminding you of Taillandy, are you?"

"Heavens, no! He reminds me of nothing at all. Nothing, I tell you! He isn't witty . . ."

"People in love are always a bit idiotic. Take me, for instance, when I was in love with Jeanne . . ."

"Not to mention me, when I was in love with Adolphe! But that was a conscious idiocy, almost voluptuous. Do you remember the evenings when we dined out, Adolphe and I, and I would put on my poor look, my 'look of a dowerless daughter', as Margot used to say? My husband held forth, smiled, laid down the law and shone. No one had eyes for anyone but him. If anyone cast a glance at me I am sure it was to pity him. I was made to understand so well that, without him, I didn't exist."

"Oh, come now, that's a bit exaggerated."

"Not very much, Hamond! Don't protest! I whole-heartedly tried to efface myself as much as possible. I was so fatuously in love with him!"

"I was just the same, just the same!" says Hamond, warming up. "D'you remember when my small chit of a Jeanne used to give her opinion on my pictures? 'Henri was born conscientious and old-fashioned', she would declare. And I never said a word."

We laugh and feel happy, rejuvenated by this stirring up of humiliating and bitter memories. Why must my old friend spoil this Saturday, so much in harmony with all our traditions, by bringing in the name of Dufferein-Chautel?

I make a cross face. "There you go again! Do give me a bit of a rest from that gentleman, Hamond! What do I know about him? That he's clean, well brought up, is fond of bull-dogs and smokes cigarettes. That he happens, into the bar-gain, to be in love with me is not—to be modest—a very special characteristic."

"But you do everything in your power never to get to know him!"

"Well, I have every right."

That irritates Hamond, who clucks his tongue disapprov-ingly: "Your right, your right! My dear friend, you argue like a child, I do assure you!"

I take away my hand, which he had covered with his own, and speak fast, in spite of myself: "You do assure me of what? That he's a gilt-edged security? What is it you really want? That I should go to bed with this gentleman?"

"Renée!"

"Well, one might as well say it! You want me to act like everyone else? To make up my mind? Him or someone else, what's it matter! You want to upset my newly-recovered peace, to make me exchange the keen, invigorating, natural care of earning my own living for a care of a different kind? Or per-haps you're advising me to take a lover for health reasons, as a blood-purifier? But what for? I'm in good health and, thank God, I love no one, no one, and never again will I love anyone, anyone, anyone!"

I shouted that so loud that all of a sudden I fall silent, quite abashed. Hamond, who is not so carried away as I, gives me time to get a grip on myself while my blood, which had risen to my cheeks, runs slowly back to my heart.

"You'll never again love anyone? Alas, that may be true! And that would be saddest of all. To think of you, young and strong, and affectionate. . . . Yes, that would be saddest of all."

Indignant, and on the verge of tears, I gaze at the friend who dares to speak thus to me: "Oh Hamond, can it be you who say that to me! After what has happened to you . . . to us, could you still hope for love?"

Hamond turns away his gaze, stares at the window with those eyes that are so young in his old face, and replies vaguely: "Yes. It's true I'm very happy as I am. But just because of that, to answer for myself and definitely say: 'I shall never love again,' good lord no, I wouldn't dare!"

That strange answer from Hamond put an end to our discussion, for I don't like talking of love. The broadest of broad jokes doesn't scare me, but I don't like talking of love. If I had lost a beloved child, it seems to me that I should never again be able to pronounce its name.

f o u r

"COME AND HAVE A BITE AT OLYMPE'S THIS EVENING," SAID Brague to me at the rehearsal. "And afterwards we'll go and say hullo to the boys in the *Revue* at the *Emp'-Clich'*."

There's no danger of my misunderstanding: this is not an *invitation* to dinner; we are two *comrades*, and the protocol—for there is one—governing comradeship between artistes banishes all ambiguity.

So I rejoin Brague this evening at Olympe's bar, whose doubtful reputation does not in the least disturb me. Now that I need give no thought to my own reputation, I feel neither apprehension nor pleasure when I enter this little Montmartre restaurant, which is silent from seven to ten and resounds all the rest of the night with what seems rather a deliberate din made up of shouts, the clatter of crockery and the twanging of guitars. I sometimes used to go and dine there in haste, alone or with Brague, last month, before we went on to the *Empyrée-Clichy*.

This evening a waitress from the country, tranquil and slow in the midst of the calls for her, serves us with pickled pork and cabbage, a filling, nourishing dish, rather heavy for the stomachs of the poor little local prostitutes who sit eating near us, by themselves, with that aggressive look which animals and under-nourished women adopt when a heaped plate is put before them. No, indeed, the place is not always gay!

Brague, mocking but compassionate at heart, speaks

slightingly of two thin young women who have just entered, with idiotic hats balanced precariously on their curly heads. One of them is striking, and carries her head with a kind of angry insolence; every line of her exaggerated slenderness shows, in all its grace, beneath a tight sheath of pink Liberty silk, bought from the second-hand clothes woman. On this freezing February evening all she has to cover her is a cloak, a sort of light cape, also of Liberty silk, blue and embroidered with tarnished silver. She is frozen, almost beside herself with cold, and her furious grey eyes repulse all compassion; she is ready to insult, or even to claw, the first person who says to her, sympathetically, "Poor child!"

Young women of this kind, slowly dying of misery and pride, beautiful in their stark poverty, are by no means uncommon in this district of Montmartre. I meet them here and there, trailing their flimsy garments from table to table at supper-time on the Butte, gay, drunk, and fierce, always ready to bite, never gentle, never affectionate, resenting their profession and "working" all the same. The men call them "wretched little sluts", with a contemptuous but admiring laugh, because they belong to a breed which never gives in, never admits to cold or hunger or love; little sluts who die saying: "I'm not ill," who may bleed under blows, but hit back all the same.

Yes, I know something of those girls, and it is of them that I am reminded as I watch the proud, frozen young girl who has just come into Olympe's.

A hungry half-silence reigns in the bar. Two painted young men exchange barbed repartee from opposite ends of the room, without any conviction. A street-girl with short legs, who is dining on a crème-de-menthe with water while awaiting a problematical supper, throws out a few half-hearted retorts. A bulldog bitch, in pup to bursting point, pants painfully on the threadbare carpet, her balloon of a stomach studded with knob-like teats.

Brague and I chat, relaxed by the warmth of the gas. I think of all the mediocre restaurants in all the towns which have seen us thus seated at table, tired, indifferent and curious, before strange meats. The hog-wash of station buffets and hotel restaurants is never too much for Brague's iron stomach; but as for me, if the plain veal or the leg of mutton *bonne femme* are so leathery that they defeat me, I make up on the cheese and the omelette.

"I say, Brague, that man over there with his back to us, isn't it Stephen-the-Dancer?"

"Where? Yes, that's him all right . . . with a tart."

Such a "tart", in fact, that I remain flabbergasted at the sight of that fifty-year-old brunette with her dark moustache. And as if he felt our eyes on him, Stephen-the-Dancer half turns to throw us one of those knowing looks which are used in the theatre to convey: "Not a word! It's a mystery!" discreetly enough to be noticed by the whole house.

"Poor wretch, he certainly earns any money *he* gets," whispers Brague. "Coffee, Mademoiselle," he calls, "we've got to skedaddle."

The coffee is an olive-black ink which leaves a clinging stain on the sides of the cups. But as a result of never drinking good coffee any more, I have come to like these hot, bitter brews which smell of liquorice and quinine. In our profession we can do without meat but not without coffee.

Quickly as they serve us ours, Stephen-the-Dancer "skedaddles" before us—he is *rinking* in the *Revue* at the *Emp'-Clich'*—in the wake of his companion. Behind her back he shamelessly imitates for us the gesture of the athlete who "heaves" the four hundred pound weight, and we are cowardly enough to laugh. Then we leave this sad, so-called "pleasure" haunt, where by this time everyone is getting drowsy under the pink lights: the pregnant bitch, the exhausted street-girls, the waitress from the country and the manager with his waxed moustache.

Once outside, the outer boulevard and the Place Blanche,

round which an icy wind circles, revive us, and I feel myself joyfully seized once more with an active passion, a real need to *work*, a mysterious and undefined need which I could satisfy equally well by dancing, writing, running, acting, or pulling a handcart.

As if the same desire had seized him, Brague suddenly says to me: "By the way, I've had a word from the agent, Salomon. The tour I spoke about's taking shape. He's fixing up one day here and two there, a week in Marseilles and another in Bordeaux. You can still go?"

"Me? Right away! Why not?"

He darts a sharp sideways glance at me.

"Oh, I don't know. Sometimes a mere trifle . . . I know what life is . . ."

So that's it! My comrade remembers Dufferein-Chautel and thinks that . . . My sudden laugh, instead of undeceiving him, bewilders him still further, but this evening I feel in a gay and teasing mood, and as light-hearted as if we had set off already. Oh, how lovely to go away, to move from one place to another, to forget who I am and the name of the town which sheltered me the day before, scarcely to think, to receive and retain no impressions but that of the beautiful landscape which unfolds and changes as the train runs past, of the lead-coloured pool in which the blue sky is reflected green, and the open-work spire of a belfry encircled with swallows.

I remember a day, a May morning, when I was leaving Rennes. The train very slowly followed a track under repair between coppices of white hawthorn, pink appletrees which cast a blue shadow, and very young willows with leaves of jade. A child, standing at the edge of the wood, watched us pass, a little girl of twelve whose resemblance to myself struck me. A serious child with frowning brows, and tanned round cheeks—as mine were—, and hair a little bleached by the sun, she was holding a leafy shoot in her sunburnt hands covered with scratches—as mine were. Her unsociable look, too, and those ageless, almost sexless, eyes which seemed to take everything seriously, were mine also, really mine. It was indeed my own shy childhood which stood there, dazzled by the sun, at the edge of that coppice and watched me pass.

"Whenever you like, then!"

My comrade's curt invitation brings me back to earth in front of the *Emp'-Clich'*, glittering with mauve lights, whose glare, as Brague says, hurts "the back of your eyes." We descend to the basement, where the familiar smell of plaster, ammonia, *Crème Simon* and rice-powder, rouses in me a disgust that is almost pleasant. We've come to see our pals in the *Revue*, we have, and not the *Revue* itself!

I find my old dressing-room, at present inhabited by Bouty, and Brague's, which is now filled with the dazzling presence of Jadin who is playing three parts in the *Emp'-Clich'-Revue*.

"Stir your stumps!" she calls to us. "You're just in time for my song, *Night-time in Paris*."

Alas, they have dressed Jadin as a street-walker! A black skirt, a low-cut black bodice, cobweb-fine stockings, a red ribbon round her neck and, on her head, the traditional helmet-shaped wig with a blood-red camellia in it. There is not a trace left of the endearing, guttersnipe charm of that young girl with the hunched shoulder.

It was, I suppose, inevitable that they should quickly turn my sulky young apache into the ordinary little *café-concert* singer. While we exchange the "How goes it?" "What's the news?" "Things shaping?" I watch her moving about her dressing-room, and realise with a shock that Jadin walks like a tart, as all of them do, with her stomach drawn in and her chest out, that she is careful to *pitch* her voice when she speaks, and that she has not once said "Bitch!" since we arrived.

Bouty, who is to dance the inevitable cancan with her, beams at us under his silk cap and says nothing. One feels he might at any moment say "Now what about it?", and point at the little creature with a proprietary gesture. Has he at last vanquished his comrade? At any rate I guess that it is he who is making Jadin commonplace and now there they both are talking of doing a "sensational turn", very well paid, at the Crystal Palace in London!

How quickly everything changes, especially women! In a few months this one will lose nearly all her piquancy, her natural and unconscious pathos. Will that hare-brained, eighteen-year-old Jadin, so prodigal of herself and her scanty cash, suddenly reveal an upsurge of craftiness, the craftiness of concierges and grasping small tradesmen? Why in her presence am I reminded of the Bells, German acrobats with an English name, whom Brague and I knew in Brussels? Of unequalled strength and grace in their cerise tights which made their fair skin look paler still, the five of them lived in two rooms without furniture, where they cooked for themselves on a little iron stove. And all day long, the impresario told us, it was nothing but mysterious discussions, consulting of financial newspapers, and fierce disputes concerning gold-mines, railway shares and the Egyptian Land Loan. Money, money, money.

Jadin's empty chatter enlivens our visit, which needs enlivening. After Bouty, who is slightly less thin, has given us news of his health and announced that "things are shaping" for the following winter, we fall silent and embarrassed, chance friends whom chance has separated. I fiddle with the grease-paint and pencils on the little shelf, with that greedy exasperation, that itch for make-up, familiar to anyone who has ever trodden the boards. Fortunately, the little bell tinkles and Jadin jumps to her feet: "Look sharp, up we go! The fireman'll give you his stage-box and you'll see what a hit I make in my *Night-time in Paris* song."

The sleepy fireman does in fact lend me his straw-bottomed stool and his little box. Sitting there, with my nose to the grating which frames a square of warm, reddish light, I can see, without myself being seen, half of two rows of the stalls and three uncurtained boxes, as well as a stage-box. In this stage-box I can make out a lady in an enormous hat, with pearls, rings and sequins, and two men who are Dufferein-Chautel senior and Dufferein-Chautel junior, both of them looking very black and white, and very sleek and smart. They are relentlessly illuminated and, framed by my grating, they take on an extraordinary importance.

The woman is not a woman, she is a *lady:* Madame Dufferein-Chautel senior, no doubt. My admirer, for his part, seems to be greatly amused by the march past of the girl rag-pickers, and of the girl cabbies who follow them and, after singing a couplet, dance casually off.

Finally comes Jadin, who announces herself: "And I—I am the Queen of Night-time Paris: I am the Street Walker!"

I see my admirer bend rather eagerly over the programme and then raise his head and study my little comrade closely, from her helmet of hair to her open-work stockings.

By a curious transposition, he it is who becomes the spectacle for me, for I can only see little Jadin in profile; the blinding footlights make her face look like a skull, with black nostrils and a lip foreshortened above a gleaming row of teeth, as if her face had been eaten by the light. With her neck stretched out gargoyle-fashion, a red rag knotted round it, this young girl suddenly resembles some lewd spectre by Félicien Rops.

When, at the end of her number, she twice returns to take her call, her heels together and her fingers to her lips, my admirer claps her with his big brown hands so loudly that, before she disappears, she throws him a little kiss all for himself, with a forward thrust of her chin.

"What's the matter, are you asleep? This is the second time I've told you that you can't stay there; they're setting the scene for Heliopolis!"

"All right, all right, I'm coming."

I think in fact that I must have fallen asleep, or else I am just emerging from one of those moments when one's mind goes blank before some painful idea is set in motion, moments which are the prelude to a slight loss of morale.

f i v e

"COME ON NOW, EITHER MAKE UP YOUR MIND OR DON'T. Does it seem to you all right, or doesn't it?"

There they both are, Brague and Salomon, harrying me with their looks and their voices. Salomon laughs to reassure me, while Brague keeps muttering. Then Salomon lays his heavy hand on my shoulder and says: "As contracts go, it's pretty good, I think!"

I have the typed contract in my hand, and I re-read it for the tenth time for fear there may be some hidden snare, some suspicious clause, lurking among its fifteen short lines. Above all I re-read it to gain time. And then I look at the window, the curtains of starched net, and behind them the sad, clean courtyard.

I look as if I am reflecting, but I am not reflecting. Hesitating is not reflecting. Absentmindedly, I examine the contents of the English-type desk I have seen so many times before, covered with foreign photographs: half-length portraits of ladies in low-necked frocks, with Viennese smiles; men in evening dress who might equally well be singers or acrobats, clowns or ringmasters—impossible to say which.

A six weeks tour at a hundred and fifty francs a day, that makes six thousand francs. Pretty good. But . . .

"But," I finally say to Salomon, "I don't want to put six hundred francs in your fat purse. Ten per cent, all said and done, is sheer murder."

I have found my voice again and the art of using it, and the right vocabulary for the occasion. Salomon turns the colour of his hair, brick-red; even his shifty eyes go bloodshot, but from his full, pleasant mouth pours a flood of almost amorous supplications.

"My darling, my pet, don't start saying silly things. I've been working at your itinerary for a month now, a whole month. Ask Brague! For a month I've been wearing myself out to find first-class houses for you, absolutely first-class. And posters like . . . like Madame Otéro, think of it! And that's the way you thank me! Haven't you got a heart? Ten per cent? Why it's twelve, not ten, you ought to give me, d'you hear?"

"Yes, I hear. But I don't want to put six hundred francs in your fat purse. You aren't worth such a sum."

Salomon's little red eyes grow smaller still. The heavy hand caressing my shoulder would like to crush me.

"Oh, you ungrateful wretch! Look at her, Brague! A child who owed her first engagement to me!"

"A child who's now jolly well of age, my friend, and in need of some new clothes. D'you realise my costume for *The Pursuit* is worn out? Thirty pounds for a character costume, plus the slippers, plus the veil for my dance—all the accessories, in short. You're not going to pay me for all those separately, are you, old skinflint?"

"Look at her Brague!" repeats Salomon. "I feel ashamed for her in front of you. Whatever will you think of her?"

"I think," says Brague tranquilly, "that she would be right to accept the tour and wrong to give you six hundred francs."

"All right then. Give me back the papers."

The fat hand lets go of me. Frowning and pale, Salomon goes back to his English-style desk without a glance at us.

"Come now, Salomon, let's stop pretending. I'm an absolute bitch when I want to be, and if anyone irritates me I don't care a fig if the whole thing goes down the drain!"

"Madame," answers Salomon, very dignified and stiff, "you've spoken to me as though you despised me, and I've taken it to heart."

"Silly ass!" interrupts Brague, without raising his voice. "Stop playing the fool! Six hundred for her share, four hundred and forty for mine . . . d'you take us for German acrobats? Give me the forms; we aren't going to sign today. I want twenty-four hours to consult my family."

"In that case, it's up the spout," splutters Salomon excitably. "All those people are directors of very smart houses, people who don't like being trifled with, people . . ."

"Yes, yes, I know, who go up in smoke if you cross them," interrupts my comrade. "All right, then, tell them I'll be back tomorrow. Coming, Renée? Salomon, it's seven and a half per cent for the two of us. And I call that big and generous."

Salomon wipes his dry eyes and his damp forehead.

"There you go again, I still think you're a pretty pair of sharpers."

"Well, Salomon, I can't say you're so very handsome yourself."

"Leave him alone, Renée, he's a dear creature really. He'll do as we want. In the first place, he loves you. Don't you, Salomon?"

But Salomon is sulking. He turns his back like a big child and says in a tearful voice: "No. Take yourselves off. I don't want to see you any more. I'm really hurt. It's the very first time, since I started to book engagements, that anyone has inflicted such a humiliation on me. Off with you! I want to be alone. I don't want to see you any more."

"Right you are. Till tomorrow!"

"No, no! It's all over between us three."

"Five o'clock?"

Seated at his desk, Salomon lifts his tearful pink face towards us. "Five o'clock? Well I'm blowed, I suppose I must now miss my rendezvous at the Alhambra for you? Not before six, d'you hear?"

Disarmed, I squeeze his stubby fist, and we leave.

The street is so crowded that conversation is impossible, so we are silent. I dread the comparative solitude of the

Boulevard Malesherbes, where Brague will begin to argue and convince me. I am convinced in advance and have made up my mind to go. Hamond will not be pleased. Margot will say to me: "You're quite right, my girl!" though she will be quite sure I am not, but she will give me excellent advice, and three or four boxes of "specialities" against headaches, fever and constipation.

And to come down to Dufferein-Chautel, what will he say? It amuses me to think of his face. He will console himself with Jadin, that's all. And I shall depart . . . already I begin to ask how soon.

"What was the date, Brague? I paid no attention to that, just fancy!"

Brague shrugs his shoulders and stands close to me among the cluster of pedestrians waiting submissively until the white baton cleaves the line of carriages, and opens a passage for us from the pavement of the Boulevard Haussmann to the island on the Place Saint-Augustin.

"If we had to depend on you to button up the engagements, my poor friend! Madame rants, and mounts her high horse, Madame wants this, won't have that, and then, at the end of it all, 'Fancy, I paid no attention to the date!'"

Deferentially, I let him enjoy his superiority. It is one of Brague's keenest pleasures to treat me as a novice, a blundering pupil. Protected by the policeman's baton, we hurry as far as the Boulevard Malesherbes.

"From April 5th to May 15th," finishes Brague. "You've nothing against that? Nothing to keep you?"

"Nothing."

We walk up the boulevard, panting a little because of the steam which rises from the damp pavement as from a warm bath. The thaw has set in with a slight, almost stormy, shower; the lights are reflected, elongated and iridescent, in the blackish pavement. The top of the avenue is lost to view in a blurred mist, faintly rosy in the lingering dusk. Involuntarily I look back and all about me, searching for . . . what?

Nothing. No, nothing keeps me here, or elsewhere. No dear face will rise from the mist, like a flower emerging from dark water, to beg tenderly: "Don't go away!"

So I shall leave, once again. The fifth of April is a long way off—it is now February 15th—but it is as if I had already left, and I pay no heed as Brague lists in my ear the names of towns and hotels and figures, figures, figures. . . .

"Are you at least listening to me?"

"Yes."

"So you're not doing anything between now and April 5th?"

"Not that I know of!"

"You wouldn't consider a little act, just any kind of little silly thing, something rather elegant, to occupy you between now and then?"

"My goodness, no."

"If you like, I'll look for a little weekly engagement for you?"

I thank my comrade, on parting from him, because I feel touched that he should want to save me from hard times and the idleness which demoralises out-of-work actors, diminishing their powers and making them go to pieces.

Three heads are raised when I enter my study: Hamond's, Fossette's, and Dufferein-Chautel's. All three huddled round a little table under the pink lampshade, they were playing *écarté* while they waited for me. Fossette knows how to play cards in the bulldog manner: perched on a chair, she follows the come and go of hands, ready to seize as it flies past any card thrown too far.

Hamond cries "At last!", Fossette "Wuff!", and Dufferein-Chautel says nothing, but he very nearly barked too.

To leave the fetid fog outside, for this joyful welcome under the softly-shaded light, so raises my spirits that in a burst of affectionate joy I cry: "Greetings! What d'you think, I'm going away!"

"You're going away? How d'you mean? When?"

In spite of himself a slightly curt and inquisitorial note has crept into my admirer's voice; but I pay no attention to that as I roll up my gloves and take off my hat.

"I'll tell you all about it over dinner. You'll both stay: it's almost a farewell dinner already. Stay where you are and go on with your little game; I'll send Blandine to get some cutlets and go and slip into a dressing-gown; I'm worn out!"

When I return, enveloped in the folds of a rose-coloured flannel kimono, I notice that both Hamond and Dufferein-Chautel have the too-casual look of people who have been plotting something. What does it matter? My adorer this evening is reaping the benefit of an optimism which embraces every living thing: I invite him to offer us some of the Saint-Marceaux from the grocer next door, to "drink to the tour", and he runs off at once without his hat, returning with two bottles under his arm.

Feeling feverish and a little tipsy, I bend on my admirer a trustful look which he has never seen on my face before. I laugh aloud with a laugh he has never heard, I roll the wide sleeves of my kimono back to my shoulder, revealing arms which he says are "the colour of a peeled banana". I feel kind and gentle, and for two pins I would offer him my cheek: what does it matter? I'm going away, I shall never see this young man again! It's only for forty days? Oh, but we shall certainly all be dead by the time they're over!

Poor admirer, how badly I've treated him, all the same! Now he seems to me pleasant, clean, well-groomed, and considerate . . . like someone one will never see again! For when I come back I shall have forgotten him, and he too will have forgotten me . . . with little Jadin, or with someone else. But more likely with little Jadin.

"I say, what about that little Jadin!"

I have uttered this remark, which seems to me extremely funny, at the top of my voice. My admirer, who finds it difficult to laugh this evening, wrinkles his coal-miner's eye-brows as he looks at me: "What d'you mean, that little Jadin?"

"She rather took your fancy the other day, didn't she? At the *Emp'-Clich'?*"

Dufferein-Chautel bends towards me, intrigued. As his face emerges from the zone of shadow cast by the lampshade, I can see the exact shade of his brown eyes, tawny and gold-flecked like certain agates from the Dauphiné.

"Were you in the audience? I didn't see you."

I empty my glass before replying, mysteriously: "Ah, you see!"

"Well, well, so you were there! Yes, she's charming, is little Jadin. You know her? I find her very charming."

"More than me?"

This imprudent, idiotic remark, so unworthy of me, might well have deserved a different reply from the astonished silence with which he greeted it. I could have kicked myself. Oh well, what does it matter? I'm going away! I describe my itinerary: a complete tour of France, but only the big towns! Posters like . . . like Madame Otéro! And the lovely places I shall see, and the sun I shall find in the South, and . . . and . . .

The champagne—three glasses, but that is quite enough—finally lulls my happy chatter. What an expenditure of energy talking is for someone who remains silent for days together! My two friends are smoking now, and slowly, slowly, they recede behind their veil of smoke. How far away I feel, as if I had already left, cut adrift, and taken refuge in my journey! Their voices grow muffled and fade into the distance, mingling with the rumbling of trains, with whistlings and the lulling swell of an imaginary orchestra. Ah, what a delicious departure, what a sweet sleep, which wafts me towards an invisible shore!

"Hullo? is it six o'clock? Good, thank you. . . . Ah, it's you?"

I was asleep and dreaming of the journey: a hotel servant

was knocking with his fist against the door of my dream, and calling out that it was six o'clock. And I come to, sitting up with a start in the hollow of my old divan where weariness and my slight tipsiness have made me doze off. Standing beside me, the Big-Noodle looms as high as the room. My eyes, opened too soon, blink at the lamp; the edges of the lamp-shade and the corners of the lighted table are like gleaming blades which wound my sight.

"It's you? Where's Hamond?"

"Hamond's just gone."

"What time is it then?"

"It's midnight."

"Midnight!"

I've slept for more than an hour! Mechanically I push up my flattened hair, combing it with my fingers, and then pull down my dressing-gown to the very tips of my bedroom slippers.

"Midnight? Why didn't you leave with Hamond?"

"We were afraid you might feel alarmed at finding yourself alone here. So I stayed."

Is he making fun of me? His face is so far above me in the shadow that I can't make it out.

"I was tired, you understand."

"I understand very well."

What is the meaning of this curt and scolding tone? I am quite staggered. Really, if I were easily frightened, this might seem just the moment to call for help, finding myself alone with this black-visaged creature addressing me from such a height! Perhaps he has been drinking, too.

"I say, Dufferein-Chautel, are you ill?"

"I'm not ill."

Thank goodness, he begins to move about; I had had enough of seeing him towering so close to me!

"I'm not ill, I'm angry."

"Oh, that's it!"

I consider for a moment, and then add, stupidly enough: "Is it because I'm going away?"

97

Dufferein-Chautel stops short.

"Because you're going away? I never gave it a thought. Since you're still here, there's no need for me to think that you're going away. No. I'm cross with you. I'm cross with you because you were sleeping."

"Really?"

"It's crazy to fall asleep like that! Before Hamond, and even before me! It's obvious you've no idea how you look when you're asleep. Unless you do it on purpose, and that's unworthy of you."

He sits down abruptly, as though he were breaking himself in three, and this brings him close to me, with his face on a level with mine.

"When you sleep you don't look as though you were asleep. You look . . . well, to be frank, you look as though you had closed your eyes to hide a joy that is too much for you. You really do. You haven't the face of a woman asleep, you . . . well, damn it, you know very well what I'm trying to say! It's revolting. When I think that you must have slept in that way before a heap of people, I don't know what I couldn't do to you!"

He is seated sideways on a flimsy chair, and he half turns away his distracted face, divided by two great wrinkles, one on his forehead and the other running down his cheek, as though the explosion of his wrath had just cracked him. I am not afraid; on the contrary, it is a relief to me to find him sincere, like the man who entered my dressing-room two months earlier.

Once again, then, there reappears before me, with his childish rage, his bestial persistence, his calculated sincerity, my enemy and my tormentor: love. There is no mistaking it. I have already seen that forehead, those eyes, and those hands convulsively gripping each other, yes, I have seen all that . . . in the days when Adolphe Taillandy desired me.

But what am I going to do with this one? I am not offended, I am not even moved—or only a very little! but what am I going to do? How shall I answer him? This continuing silence becomes more embarrassing than his avowal. If only he would go away . . . but he does not budge. I dare not risk the slightest movement, for fear a sigh, or a ripple of my gown, might be enough to rouse my adversary; I no longer dare say my admirer, no, he loves me too much.

"That's all you have to say to me?"

The sound of his voice, softened, causes me such keen pleasure that I smile with relief at being released from the suffocating silence.

"Well, I really don't see . . ."

He turned towards me with the clumsy gentleness of a big dog.

"That's quite true, you don't see. You have an absolute talent for not seeing. Whenever I'm concerned, you don't see, you see nothing. You look through me, you smile above my head, you speak to one side of me. And I act as though I didn't see that you don't see. How clever that is! And how worthy of you and of me!"

"Listen, Dufferein-Chautel . . ."

"And you call me Dufferein-Chautel! I know very well I've got a ridiculous name, the sort of name for a member of Parliament or an industrialist, or a director of a discount bank. It isn't my fault. All right, go on, laugh! It's a bit of luck, anyway," he adds in a lower tone, "that I can make you laugh."

"Well, then, what d'you want me to call you? Dufferein or Chautel? Or Duduffe? Or . . . just Maxime, or Max? I say, do pass me the hand-mirror, there, on the little table, and the powder puff: I must look a sight, what with the champagne, and sleeping, and no powder on my nose."

"That doesn't matter," he says impatiently. "Whoever d'you want to put powder on for, at this hour?"

"For myself, in the first place. And then for you."

"There's no need to bother on my account. You treat me like a man who is paying court to you. What if I were, quite simply, a man who loves you?"

I look at him, more distrustful than ever before, disconcerted to find in this man, as soon as it is a question of love between us, a remarkable intelligence and ease which his Big-Noodle-like appearance entirely belies. What I divine in him is, in fact, an aptitude for love, by virtue of which he both surpasses and embarrasses me.

"Tell me frankly, Renée, is it hateful, or a matter of indifference, or vaguely agreeable to you to know that I love you?"

He is neither insulting, nor humble, nor plaintive, nor is there anything timid or cunning about him. Copying his simplicity, I pluck up courage to reply: "I simply don't know." "That's just what I thought," he said gravely. "Well then . . ."

"Well then?"

"There's nothing for me to do but to go away."

"It's half an hour after midnight."

"No, you haven't understood me. What I mean is: not to see you any more, to leave Paris."

"Leave Paris? Why?" I say, simply. "There's no need for that. And I haven't forbidden you to see me again."

He shrugs his shoulders.

"Oh, I know myself! When things aren't going well, when I have . . . well, worries, I go off home."

There was something provincial and tender in the way he said "home".

"Is it pretty, where you live?"

"Yes. It's forest land. Lots of firs and quite a few oaks. I love the new fellings, you know, when they've thinned out the woods, and all that remains is the saplings and the great circles left by the charcoal fires, where wood strawberries will grow the next summer."

"And lilies of the valley . . ."

"And lilies of the valley. And foxgloves too. You know? They're as tall as that, and when you're a kid you poke your fingers in the bells."

"I know."

He describes it badly, my wood-cutter from the Ardennes, but I see so well what he describes!

"I motor down there during the summer. I shoot a little too, in the autumn. It's mother's house, of course. Mother Ever-Cut!" says he, laughing. "She cuts and cuts and saws and sells."

"Oh!"

"But she doesn't damage anything, you know. She knows what wood is, she's as knowledgeable about it as a man, better than a man."

I listen to him with a new attraction, glad that he should forget me for a moment, and that he should talk, like a worthy wood-cutter, of his mother's forest. I had not remembered that he was from the Ardennes, and he had not bothered to inform me that he loved his country-side. Now I know why he has the look of a noodle! It is because he wears his clothes rather as if they were "party clothes", with an ineradicable and endearing awkwardness, like a handsome peasant in his Sunday best.

". . . Only, if you send me away, Renée, my mother will understand at once that I have come for her to 'look after' me, and she'll want once again to get me married. Look what you're exposing me to!"

"Let yourself get married."

"You don't say that seriously?"

"Why not? Because I've had an unfortunate experience myself? What does that prove? You ought to get married, it would suit you very well. You look married already. Though you're a bachelor, you have all the appearance of a young father of a family, you adore a fireside, you're affectionate and jealous and obstinate, as lazy as a spoilt husband, a despot at heart, and monogamous from birth!"

Stupefied, my admirer stares at me without saying a word, then leaps to his feet.

"I'm all that!" he cries. "I'm all that! She's said it! I'm all that!"

I coldly check his cries and gestures.

"Do be quiet! What's possessed you? Why should being . . . well, egoistical, and lazy, and a fireside-lover make you want to dance?"

He sits down again opposite me, very meekly, but his sheep-dog's eyes rest on me with a look of victorious sagacity.

"No. It doesn't matter a bit to me that I am all you say: what makes me want to dance is the fact that you know it!"

Ah, fool that I am! There he is, triumphant, encouraged by my confession, the confession of my curiosity, if not of a sharper interest. There he is, arrogant, trembling with the longing to reveal himself further. If he dared, he would cry: "Yes, I am all that! So you have deigned to see me, while I was losing hope that I should ever exist in your eyes? Look at me again! Reveal me completely, invent weaknesses and absurdities in me, overwhelm me with imaginary vices! My worry is not that you should know me as I am: create your admirer according to your liking, and afterwards, artfully and little by little, I will make myself resemble him, as a master touches up and re-does the mediocre work of a beloved pupil."

Shall I speak my thought aloud to him to embarrass him? Careful! I nearly did another clumsy thing. He will not be embarrassed, he will listen, ravished, to his soothsayer, and praise to the skies the second sight that love confers. And what is he waiting for now? For me to fall into his arms? Nothing astonishes a man in love. I could wish him far off. I'm struggling with the need to rest, to relax, to raise my hand and beg: "Pax! Stop! I don't know the game. If I find I want to, we'll begin again another time; but I haven't the strength to follow you, and I shall get caught every time, as you well see."

His watchful eyes dart rapidly from my eyelids to my mouth, from my mouth to my eyelids, and seem to read my face. Suddenly he rises and turns aside, with brusque discretion.

"Goodbye, Renée," he says in a lower voice. "I ask your

pardon for staying so late, but Hamond suggested to me . . ."

With a sense of social embarrassment, I protest: "Oh, it doesn't matter at all . . . on the contrary . . ."

"Does your concierge sleep very soundly?"

"I hope not."

This is so pitifully silly that I recover some of my gaiety.

"Listen!" I say suddenly. "I would rather you didn't waken the concierge: you shall leave by the window."

"By the window? Oh, Renée!"

"It's the ground floor."

"I know. But aren't you afraid that . . . that I shall be seen? One of the other tenants might return just at that moment."

"Whatever d'you suppose that would matter to me?"

In spite of myself, there is so much contemptuous indifference in the way I answered him and shrugged my shoulders, that my admirer no longer dares to rejoice. In his heart, this exit at one in the morning by the window—from my bedroom, if you please—must make him feel as gleeful as a student. Ah, what youthfulness!

"Jump! That's right. Goodbye!"

"Till tomorrow, Renée?"

"If you like, my friend."

What youthfulness! Yet he is thirty-three, this man. I too. Thirty-four in six months.

I heard him running along the pavement, under a fine, clinging rain which makes the paving stones sticky and moistens the window-sill where I remain propped on my elbows, like a lover. But, behind me, no one has rumpled the big, commonplace bed, with its fresh, uncreased sheets on which my uncomplaining insomnia will leave no trace.

He has gone. He will return tomorrow, and the following days, since I have given him permission. He will return almost happy, awkward but full of hope, with that look as though he were saying: "I'm not asking for anything", which, in the end, has the same exasperating effect on me as the mechanical prayer of a beggar. And to think it would have been so simple to wound him with a refusal before he had got to the dangerous stage, and to let him go while the cut was fresh and curable!

The thin rain, falling past the square of my lighted window, looks like damp, finely-sifted flour, white against the black background of the road.

I must confess that, in allowing this man to return tomorrow, I was giving way to my desire to keep, not an admirer, not a friend, but an eager spectator of my life and my person. "One has to get terribly old," said Margot to me one day, "before one can give up the vanity of living in the presence of someone else."

Could I sincerely declare that, for a few weeks past, I have not taken pleasure in the attention of this passionate spectator? I denied him my brightest look, my freest smile; I was careful of the tone of my voice when I spoke to him, and my whole face remained closed against him. But was it not so that, distressed and humbled, he should realise that all my reticences were addressed to him, and that for his sake I was taking the trouble to exist less? There is no disguise without coquetry, and it needs as much care and vigilance to make oneself ugly all the time as to adorn oneself.

If my admirer, in the shadow, is watching my open window, he has reason to be proud. I am neither regretting him nor wanting him, but I am thinking of him. I am thinking of him as though I were taking stock of my first defeat.

The first? No, the second. There was an evening—oh, what a bitter memory, and how I curse it for rising up at this moment—an evening when, propped on my elbows like this, I was leaning out over an invisible garden. My long, long hair hung down from the balcony like a silk rope. The certainty of love had just swooped down on me, and, far from weakening under it, my young strength bore it proudly. Neither doubt, nor even the sweetest melancholy sobered that triumphal and solitary night, crowned with wisteria and roses. What did the man who aroused it do with that blind, that innocent exaltation?

Shut the window, shut the window! I tremble too much lest I should see rising, through the veil of the rain, a country garden, green and black, silvered by the rising moon across which passes the shadow of a young girl dreamily winding her long plait round her wrist, like a caressing snake.

s i x

"MARSEILLES, NICE, CANNES, TOULON . . ."
"No, Mentone before Toulon . . ."
"And Grenoble! We've got Grenoble too!"
We reckon up the towns of our tour like children counting their marbles. Brague has decided that we should take two "numbers": *The Pursuit* and *The Dryad*.

"For the big burgs where we do four or six days," he declares, "it's just as well to have a second string."

I readily agree to that. I readily agree to anything. No one could be kindlier and more appreciative than I am this morning. There is hardly a sound to be heard at Cernuschi's studio, where we are working, except Brague's outbursts and the laughter of the "Old Troglodyte" who is thrilled with the idea of going on tour and earning fifteen francs a day: his famished young face, with its sunken blue eyes, beams with uninterrupted happiness, and goodness knows he is paying for it!

"You fat-headed louse!" yells Brague. "Take that ballet-dancer's smirk off, can't you? Anyone'd think you'd never seen a troglodyte. Twist your mug sideways, I tell you! More still! And make your eyes start out! And your jaw quiver! Sort of like Chaliapine, that's the kind of thing."

He wipes his forehead and turns towards me, discouraged: "I can't think why I wear myself out over that clod; when I talk to him of Chaliapine, he thinks I am using rude words to him. And you too, what are you up to, gaping at the ceiling?"

"Oh, so it's my turn now? I was just saying to myself, it's a long time since Brague murmured some love-words to me."

My comrade-professor eyes me with a look of theatrical contempt: "Love-words! I leave those to others: I don't suppose you're short of them, are you? And now, off with you! The meeting's adjourned. Tomorrow, dress rehearsal with scenery and accessories, which is to say that you'll have a veil for your dance, while this gentleman here will carry a packing-case full of candles to represent the rock he brandishes over our heads. I'm tired of seeing you both, you with a handkerchief the size of one of my buttocks, and him with his *Paris-Journal* rolled into a ball instead of his lump of granite. Ten o'clock tomorrow, here. Them's my orders."

Just when Brague stops speaking, a ray of sunshine gilds the glass ceiling, and I raise my head as if I had suddenly heard someone calling me from above.

"D'you hear me, you chit of a Renée?"

"Yes."

"Yes? Well then off with you. It's time for grub. Go and wallow in the sun outside. You're dreaming of the country, isn't that it?"

"Nothing escapes you. Till tomorrow."

I'm dreaming of the country, yes, but not in the way that my infallible companion supposes. And the joyful hubbub of the Place Clichy at midday in no wise dispels a nagging memory that is still fresh and keen.

Yesterday Hamond and Dufferein-Chautel took me to the woods at Meudon, like two art-students taking out a little milliner. My admirer was showing off a new car that smelt of morocco leather and turpentine: a magnificent toy for grown-ups. His dark youthful face was alight with longing to offer me this beautiful, gleaming, vibrating object for which I had not the slightest wish. But I laughed because, for this outing to

Meudon, Hamond and Dufferein-Chautel were wearing identical wide-brimmed brown hats with a dint in the crown, and I looked so small between those two tall creatures.

Sitting opposite me on one of the tip-up seats, my admirer tucked his legs discreetly under him so that my knees should not touch his. The clear, grey day, very mild and spring-like, showed me all the details of his face, darker than ever under the bronze felt, with the smoky tone of his eyelids and the double row of stiff, thick eyelashes. His mouth, half-hidden under his rusty-black moustache, intrigued me, as did the faint network of little wrinkles below his eyes, and the thick, rather untidy eyebrows that extended beyond their orbit, bristling rather like those of hunting griffons. I suddenly began to grope, with an anxious hand, for the looking-glass in my little bag.

"Have you lost something, Renée?"

But I had already changed my mind: "No, nothing; thank you."

What would be the sense of examining, in front of him, the blemishes of a face which is losing the habit of being looked at in daylight? And what could my mirror have taught me, since yesterday, as on all other days, a skilful make-up of brown pencil, bluish kohl, and red lipstick managed to draw attention to my eyes and my mouth, the three lights, the three loadstars of my face. No rouge on my rather hollow cheeks, nor beneath the eyelids which weariness and frequent blinking have already delicately chequered.

The happiness of Fossette, who sat on my knees craning towards the door, provided us with occasional conversation, as did also the charm of that still wintry wood, with its grey twigs against a chinchilla sky. But whenever I leant forward to drink in a little of the gentle breeze, laden with the bitter musk of old, decayed leaves, I felt the gaze of my admirer dwelling confidently on my whole person.

Between Paris and the woods of Meudon we had not exchanged a hundred phrases. The country never makes me talkative, and my old Hamond feels bored as soon as he passes beyond the fortifications. Our silence might have cast a gloom over anyone but an admirer, sufficiently recompensed by the private satisfaction of having me there under his eyes, a passive prisoner in his car, vaguely enjoying the outing and smiling at the bumps in the damp and rutted road.

With a short bark, Fossette imperiously decided that we should go no further, and that some urgent business was call-ing her from the depths of those bare woods, on that forest road where the pools left by a recent downpour shone like round mirrors. We all three followed her without protest, with the long strides of people used to walking.

"It smells good," says the Big-Noodle suddenly, sniffing the air. "It smells like it does at home."

I shook my head: "No, not like *your* home, like mine! Hamond, what does it smell like?"

"It smells like autumn," says Hamond in a weary voice.

Whereupon we said no more and stood still, gazing up at a rivulet of sky imprisoned between very tall trees, and listening to the liquid call, clear and quavering, of a blackbird defying the winter, that came to us through the living, whispered mur-mur that rises from a forest.

A little red-brown creature started up from under our feet, a stoat or a weasel Fossette pretended she had put to flight, and we followed the stupid, excited bitch who kept showing off and barking: "I see it! I've got it!" as she followed an imagi-nary track.

In the end, catching the excitement, I set off after her down the path, giving myself up to the animal pleasure of the chase, my skunk cap pulled well down to my ears, and grasping my skirt in both hands to leave my legs free. When I stopped, out of breath, I found Maxime behind me.

"Oh, you followed me? Why didn't I hear you running?"

He was breathing fast, his eyes shining under his uneven eyebrows, his hair ruffled by the chase, very much the amo-rous wood-cutter and rather alarming.

109

"I followed you . . . I was careful to run at the same pace as you so that you shouldn't hear my steps. It's quite simple."

Yes, it's quite simple. But it had to be thought of. For my part I shouldn't have thought of it. Provoked and imprudent, a nymph-like brutality took possession of me and I laughed full in his face, defying him. I was tempted, and wanted to light again the wicked yellow light in the depths of those beautiful eyes flecked with grey and red-brown. The menace duly appeared in them, but I refused to yield, obstinate as a cheeky child who expects and asks for a slap. And the chastisement came, in the form of a badly-planted, irascible kiss, a bungled kiss in short, which left my mouth punished and disappointed.

As I follow the Boulevard des Batignolles, I carefully weigh all the moments of the day out yesterday, not in order to relive them complacently, nor to find an excuse. There is no excuse, except for the man whom I provoked. "How unlike me that was!" I mentally exclaimed to myself, yesterday, while we were returning towards Hamond, dissatisfied with each other and in a defiant mood. But was it? How do I know? "You have no more redoubtable enemy than yourself!" A pretended thoughtlessness, a pretended imprudence—these are to be found at the bottom of the most mischievously impulsive women, and I am not one of them. One should be severe with those of them who cry: "Oh, I no longer know what I am doing!" and realise that there is in their confusion a large admixture of premeditated cunning.

I do not at all say that I am not responsible, even partly. What shall I say to this man, this evening, if he wants to clasp me in his arms? That I do not want, that I never did want to tempt him, and that it is a game? That I offer him my friendship for the period of one month and ten days which separates us from the tour? No, the time has come to make up my mind, the time has come to make up my mind.

I walk on and on, quickening my steps every time I see my reflection in a shop window, because the expression of anxious determination which I see on my face looks to me rather too theatrical, with eyes not sufficiently in earnest under frowning brows. I know that face. It puts on a mask of austerity, of renunciation, the better to wait for the little miracle, the sign of my master, Chance, the phosphorescent word that he will write on the black wall when I turn out my light tonight.

How good the air smells round these little barrows full of wet violets and white jonquils! An old man all mossy with beard is selling up-rooted snowdrops with their bulbs clotted with earth and their pendant flowers shaped like a bee. Their scent resembles that of the orange-flower, but so faint as to be almost imperceptible.

Come now, come, the time has come to make up my mind! I walk and walk as if I did not know that, in spite of my bursts of energy, my scruples and all that inner penitence which I try to inflict on myself, as if I did not know, already, that I shall not take *that* course, but the *other!*

s e v e n

HEAVENS, HOW TIRED I AM, ABSOLUTELY WORN OUT! I FELL asleep after lunch, as I sometimes do on rehearsal days, and I've wakened up utterly weary, feeling as though I had come from the ends of the earth, astonished and sad and barely able to think, eyeing my familiar furniture with a hostile gaze. Just such an awakening, in fact, as the most horrible of those I used to experience in the days of my suffering. But since I am not suffering now, what can the reason be?

I feel unable to move. I look at my hand hanging down as though it did not belong to me. I don't recognise the stuff of my frock. Who was it, while I slept, who loosened the coronet of plaits coiled about my brows like the tresses of a grave young Ceres? I was . . . I was . . . there was a garden . . . a peach-coloured sunset sky . . . a shrill childish voice answering the cries of the swallows . . . yes, and that sound like distant water, sometimes powerful and sometimes muffled: the breath of a forest. I had gone back to the beginning of my life. What a journey to catch up with myself again, where I am now! I cry for the sleep that has fled, the dark curtain which sheltered me and now has withdrawn itself, leaving me shivering and naked. Sick people who think they are cured experience these fresh attacks of their malady which find them childishly astonished and plaintive: "But I thought it was over!" For two pins I could groan aloud, as they do.

O dangerous and too-kindly sleep which in less than an hour obliterates the memory of myself! Whence come I, and on what wings, that it should take me so long, humiliated and exiled, to accept that I am myself? Renée Néré, dancer and mime. . . . Was my proud childhood, my withdrawn and passionate adolescence, which welcomed love so fearlessly, to lead to no end but that?

O Margot, my discouraging friend, if only I had strength to get up, and run to you, and tell you. . . . But my courage is the only thing you admire and I should not dare to falter before you. I feel pretty sure that your direct gaze and the clasp of your dry little hand, chapped by cold water and household soap, would know better how to reward a victory over myself than to help me in my daily efforts.

And what of my approaching departure? And freedom? Ah, no! The only moment when freedom is truly dazzling is at the dawn of love, of first love, when you can say, as you offer it to the person you love: "Take! I wish I could give you more."

As for the new cities and new countrysides, so briefly glimpsed, so quickly passed that they grow blurred in the memory, are there such things as new countries for one who spins round and round in circles like a bird held on a string? Will not my pathetic flight, begun anew each morning, inevitably end up each evening at the fatal "first-class establishment" which Salomon and Brague praise so highly to me?

I have seen so many *first-class establishments* already! On the side of the public there is an auditorium cruelly flooded with light, where the heavy smoke hardly tones down the gilt of the mouldings. On the artistes' side there are sordid, airless cells, and a staircase leading to filthy lavatories.

Must I really, for forty days, endure this struggle against fatigue, the bantering ill-will of the stage-hands, the raging pride of provincial conductors, the inadequate fare of hotels and stations? Must I discover and perpetually renew in myself that rich fund of energy which is essential to the life of wanderers and solitaries? Must I, in short, struggle—ah, how could I forget it?—against solitude itself? And to achieve what? What? What?

When I was small they said to me: "Effort brings its own reward", and so, whenever I had tried specially hard, I used to expect a mysterious, overwhelming recompense, a sort of grace to which I should have surrendered myself. I am still expecting it.

The muffled trill of a bell, followed by the barking of my dog, delivers me at last from this bitter reverie. And suddenly I am on my feet, surprised to find I have jumped lightly up and begun quite simply to live again.

"Madame," says Blandine in a low voice, "may M. Dufferein-Chautel come in?"

"No . . . just a minute."

To powder my cheeks, redden my lips, and comb out the tangled locks which hide my forehead is a rapid mechanical task which does not even need the help of a mirror. One does it as one brushes one's nails, more for manners than vanity.

"Are you there, Dufferein-Chautel? You can come in. Wait a moment, I'll turn on the light."

I feel no embarrassment at seeing him again. The fact that our mouths met yesterday, abortively, does not make me feel the least awkward at this moment. A bungled kiss is much less important than an understanding exchange of looks. And I almost feel surprised that he for his part should look unhappy and frustrated. I called him Dufferein-Chautel as usual, as though he had no Christian name. I always call him "You" or "Dufferein-Chautel". Is it for me to put him at his ease? I suppose it is.

"So there you are! Are you well?"

"Thank you, I'm well."

"You don't look it."

"That's because I'm unhappy," he does not fail to reply.

Really, what a Big-Noodle! I smile at his unhappiness, the trifling unhappiness of a man who has embraced clumsily the woman he loves. I smile at him from rather far away, from the other side of the chaste black stream where I was bathing a while back. I hand him a little vase filled with his favourite cigarettes, made of a sweet, golden tobacco which smells like spice-bread.

"You're not smoking today?"

"Yes, of course. But I'm unhappy all the same."

Sitting on the divan, with his back against the low cushions, he exhales at regular intervals long jets of smoke from his nostrils. I smoke too, for something to do and to keep him company. He looks better bareheaded. A top-hat makes him uglier and a soft felt handsomer to the point of flashiness. He smokes with his eyes on the ceiling, as though the seriousness of the words he is preparing prevented him from paying any attention to me. His long, shining eyelashes—the one sensuous, feminine ornament of that face whose fault is excess of virility—blink frequently, betraying agitation and hesitancy. I can hear him breathing. I can also hear the tick-tock of my little travelling-clock, and the screen in the fireplace which the wind suddenly rattles.

"Is it raining outside?"

"No," he says with a start. "Why do you ask me that?"

"So's to know. I haven't been out since lunch, I don't know what the weather's like."

"Just ordinary . . . Renée!"

All of a sudden he sits up and throws away his cigarette. He takes my hands and looks very closely at me, so closely that his face appears to me almost too big, with the details strongly emphasized, the texture of the skin, and the moist and quivering corner of his large eyes. What love there is, yes, love, in those eyes! How speaking they are, and gentle, and wholly enamoured! And those big hands which clasp mine with such steady, communicative strength, how much in earnest I feel them!

It is the first time that I leave my hands in his. At first I feel I have to overcome my repugnance, then their warmth reassures and persuades me, and in a moment I shall yield to the surprising, brotherly pleasure, for so long unfamiliar, of confiding without words in a friend, of leaning for a moment against him, of finding comfort in the nearness of a warm, motionless being, affectionate and silent. Oh, to throw my arms round the neck of a creature, dog or man, a creature who loves me!

"Renée! What is it, Renée, you're not crying?"

"Am I crying?"

He's quite right, I am! The light dances in my brimming tears in a thousand broken, criss-cross rays. I wipe them quickly with a corner of my handkerchief, but I don't dream of denying them. And I smile at the idea that I was about to cry. How long is it since last I cried? It must be years and years.

My friend is overcome. He draws me towards him and forces me—not that I protest much—to sit beside him on the divan. His eyes, too, are moist. After all he is only a man, capable of feigning an emotion, no doubt, but not of hiding it.

"My darling child, what is the matter?"

Will he forget the stifled cry, the shudder which answers him? I hope so. "My darling child!" His first word of tenderness is "My darling child!" The same word and almost the same accent as *the other* . . .

A childish fear wrenches me from his arms, as if *the other* had just appeared at the door with his Kaiser William moustache, his false, veiled gaze, his terrible shoulders and his short, peasant's thighs.

"Renée, my darling, if only you would talk to me a little!"

My friend is quite pale and does not try to take me in his arms again. May he at least never know the pain he has just, so innocently, given me! I no longer want to cry. My delicious, cowardly tears slowly return to their source, leaving a burning sensation in my eyes and throat. While I wait for my voice to steady itself, I reassure my friend with a nod.

"I've made you angry, Renée?"

"No, my friend."

I sit down beside him again, of my own accord, but timidly, for fear my gesture and my words should provoke another tender exclamation as familiar and hateful as the last.

His instinct warns him not to rejoice at my sudden docility. I feel no desire to embrace me in the arm which supports me, and the dangerous, grateful communicative warmth is no longer there. No doubt he loves me enough to guess that, if I lay an obedient head on his strong shoulder, it is a question of a trial more than a gift.

Can this be my forehead on a man's shoulder? Am I dreaming? I am neither dreaming nor wandering. Both my head and my senses are calm, ominously calm. Yet there is something better and more than indifference in the ease which keeps me there, and the fact that I can let my hand play innocently and unthinkingly with the plaited gold chain on his waistcoat shows that I feel myself sheltered and protected, like the lost cat one rescues, who only knows how to play and sleep when it has a house.

Poor admirer . . . I wonder what he is thinking of as he sits there motionless, respecting my silence? I lean my head back to look at him, but immediately lower my lids, dazzled and abashed by the expression on this man's face. Ah, how I envy him for loving so deeply, for the passion that confers such beauty on him!

His eyes meet mine and he smiles bravely.

"Renée . . . do you think a time will ever come when you will love me?"

"Love you? How I wish I could, my friend! *You*, at least, don't look cruel. Don't you feel that I am beginning to get fond of you?"

"To get fond of me . . . that's just what I'm afraid of, Renée; that hardly ever leads to love."

He is so profoundly right that I do not protest.

"But . . . be patient . . . you never know. It may be that,

when I come back from my tour . . . And then, after all, a great, great friendship . . ."

He shakes his head. Obviously he has no use for my friendship. For my part I should be very glad to have a friend who was less old, less *worn out*, than Hamond, a real friend. . . .

"When you come back. . . . In the first place, if you really hoped to love me one day, Renée, you wouldn't think of going away from me. In two months' time, just as now, it will be the same Renée who will stretch out her cold little hands, with eyes that shut me out, and that mouth which, even when it offers its lips, does not surrender itself."

"It's not my fault. Yet here it is, this mouth. See . . ."

With my head on his shoulder once more, I close my eyes, more resigned than curious, only to open them again at the end of a moment, surprised that he does not swoop down with the greedy haste of yesterday. All he has done is to turn a little towards me and encircle me comfortably with his right arm. Then he gathers my two hands into his free hand and bends forward, and I see slowly approaching the serious unfamiliar face of this man whom I know so little.

Now there is hardly any space or air between our two faces, and I try and jerk myself free, breathing fast as if I were drowning. But he holds my hands and tightens his arm round my waist. In vain I bend my neck back, just at the moment when Maxime's mouth reaches mine.

I have not closed my eyes. I frown in an attempt to threaten those eyes above me, which try to subjugate and extinguish mine. For his lips which kiss me are just the same as yesterday, gentle, cool and impersonal, and their ineffectiveness irritates me. But all of a sudden they change, and now I no longer recognise the kiss, which quickens, insists, falters, then begins again with a rhythmical movement, and finally stops as if waiting for a response which does not come.

I move my head imperceptibly, because of his moustache which brushes against my nostrils with a scent of vanilla and honeyed tobacco. Oh! . . . suddenly my mouth, in spite of itself, lets itself be opened, opens of itself as irresistibly as a ripe plum splits in the sun. And once again there is born that exacting pain that spreads from my lips, all down my flanks as far as my knees, that swelling as of a wound that wants to open once more and overflow—the voluptuous pleasure that I had forgotten.

I let the man who has awakened me drink the fruit he is pressing. My hands, stiff a moment ago, lie warm and soft in his, and my body, as I lie back, strives to mould itself to his. Drawn close by the arm which holds me, I burrow deeper into his shoulder and press myself against him, taking care not to separate our lips and to prolong our kiss comfortably.

He understands and assents, with a happy little grunt. Sure at last that I shall not flee, it is he who breaks away from me, to draw breath and contemplate me as he bites his moist lips. I let my lids fall, since I no longer need to see him. Is he going to undress me and take possession of me completely? It doesn't matter. I am lapped in a lazy, irresponsible joy. The only urgent thing is that that kiss should begin again. We have all our time. Full of pride, my friend gathers me up in his arms as though I were a bunch of flowers, and half lays me on the divan where he rejoins me. His mouth tastes of mine now, and has the faint scent of my powder. Experienced as it is, I can feel that it is trying to invent something new, to vary the caress still further. But already I am bold enough to indicate my preference for a long, drowsy kiss that is almost motionless —the slow crushing, one against the other, of two flowers in which nothing vibrates but the palpitation of two coupled pistils.

119

And now comes a great truce when we rest and get our breath back. This time it was I who left him, and got up because I felt the need to open my arms, to draw myself up and stretch. Anxious to arrange my hair and see what my new face looked like, I took up the hand-mirror, and it makes me laugh to see we both have the same sleepy features, the same trembling, shiny, slightly swollen lips. Maxime has remained on the divan and his mute appeal receives the most flattering of responses: my look of a submissive bitch, rather shame-faced, rather cowed, very much petted, and ready to accept the leash, the collar, the place at her master's feet, and everything.

eight

HE HAS GONE. WE DINED TOGETHER, RATHER A SCRATCH meal; Blandine did us some cutlets in gravy, with gherkins. I was consumed with hunger. "*Et l'amour comblant tout, hormis . . .*", said he, to show he had read Verlaine.

We did not fall into each other's arms when dinner was over, and we have not become lovers, since he is shy and I dislike doing things on the spur of the moment. But I have pledged and promised myself, joyfully and without coquetry.

"We've got plenty of time, haven't we, Max?"

"Not too much, darling. I've grown so old while I've been waiting for you!"

So old! He does not know how old I am.

He has gone, and he will return tomorrow. He could hardly tear himself away from me, and I was so afraid I might weaken that I held him at arms' length. I felt warm and he sniffed me ecstatically, as though he were about to bite me. But at last he has gone. I say "at last", because now I shall be able to think about him, and about us.

"Love" was what he said. Is it love? I should like to be sure of it. Do I love him? My sensuality frightened me; but perhaps it will prove to be only a moment of crisis, an overflowing of forces pent up for such a long time, and afterwards no doubt I shall find I love him. What if he were to come back and knock on my shutter? Yes, certainly I love him. I brood tenderly over the memory of certain inflexions in his voice today—the echo of his little amorous grunt is enough to make me catch my breath—and then how good and strong he was, and what a comfort in my solitude when I laid my head on his shoulder! Oh yes, I do love him. What is it that has made me so timorous? I did not make so much fuss when . . .

Imprudently my train of thought has stumbled on a grave. Too late to flee, I find myself once again face to face with that pitiless mentor who speaks to me from the other side of the looking-glass:

"You didn't make so much fuss when love swept down on you and found you so mad and brave. You didn't ask yourself, that day, *if it was love*. You couldn't mistake it; it was love indeed, *first love*. That was what it was and never again will be. Your maiden simplicity recognised love without hesitation, and begrudged him neither your body nor your childish heart. It was then love made his appearance unannounced, unchosen, unquestioned. And never again will it be he. He took from you what you can only give once: trust, the religious wonder of the first caress, the novelty of your tears, the flower of your first suffering. Love, if you can; no doubt this will be granted you, so that at the summit of your poor happiness you may again remember that nothing counts, in love, except the first love, and endure at every moment the punishment of remembering, and the horror of comparing. Even when you say: 'Ah, this is better!' you will feel the pang of knowing that nothing which is not unique is good. There is a God who says to the sinner: 'You would not seek me if you had not already found me!' But Love is not so merciful. 'You, who have found me once,' he says, 'you shall lose me for ever!' Did you think, when you lost him, that you had reached the limit of suffering? It is not over yet. In striving now to be again what once you were, you will realise the height from which you fell; and the first, the only love will instil its poison into each feast of your new life, if you do not stem its flow."

n i n e

I SHALL HAVE TO SPEAK TO MARGOT AND TELL HER OF THIS event, this touch of the sun which sets my life aflame. For it has come to that, we love each other. It has come to that and, besides, I have made up my mind to it. I have sent to the devil all my memories-and-regrets, and my obsession about what I call sentimental high-water marks, and my *ifs* and *fors* and *buts* and *howevers*.

We spend every moment together, he sweeps me off my feet, dazes me with his presence and prevents me from thinking. He decides, he almost commands, and I surrender to him not only my liberty but my pride too, since I let him fill my flat with a wasteful abundance of flowers and of next summer's fruits, and I wear a little glittering arrow, pinned against my neck as though it were driven into my throat, all bleeding with rubies.

And yet we are not lovers. Max has grown patient now, and imposes on himself and me a curiously exhausting period of betrothal which in less than a week has already made us languid and slightly thinner. It is not vice in him which makes him act thus, but the coquetry of a man who wants to make himself desired and, at the same time, leave me an illusory "free will" for as long as I want.

In any case there is not much left for me to desire. And the only thing which makes me tremble at present is that unsuspected ardour which leapt into life at the first contact and is always fiercely ready to obey him. I agree he is right to postpone the hour which will unite us completely. I know my value now, and the splendour of the gift which he will receive. I shall surpass his wildest hopes, I am sure of it. In the meantime let him cull a little of the fruit in his orchard if he wants.

And he does often want. For my pleasure and to my disturbance chance has willed that in this tall young man, with his straightforward, symmetrical good looks, there is a subtle lover, born for women, and so skilled at divining that his caresses seem to know the thoughts behind my desire. He makes me think—and I blush for it—of the saying of a lascivious little music-hall comrade who boasted of the cleverness of a new lover: "My dear, one couldn't do better oneself!"

But . . . I shall have to let Margot know! Poor Margot, whom I was forgetting. As for Hamond, he has disappeared. He knows everything, thanks to Max, and keeps away from my house like a discreet relation.

And Brague! I can't forget how he looked at our last rehearsal. He greeted me on my arrival in Max's car with his best Pierrot's grimace, but he still says nothing. He even displayed an unusual and undeserved courtesy, for that morning I was blundering and absentminded, and kept blushing and excusing myself. Finally he burst out: "Be off with you! Go back to it! Take your fill and don't come back here till you've had all you can take!"

The more I laughed, the more he fulminated, looking like a little oriental fiend: "Laugh away, go on, laugh! If you could see the look on your face!"

"My look?"

"Yes, a look that's absolutely asking for it, craving for it. Don't raise your eyes to me, Messalina! Look at her," he cried, calling invisible gods to witness, "she shows those orbs there in broad daylight. And when I ask her to put that much and a bit more too into the Dryad's love scene, and to hot the whole thing up a bit, she trots out the chilly charm of a young girl at her first communion."

* * *

"Does *that* really show?" I asked Max, who was taking me home. The same mirror which the other evening reflected a countenance glorying in its defeat, now frames a pointed face with the defiant smile of a friendly fox. Yet an indefinable flame keeps flickering over it, painting it, as it were, with a kind of tormented youthfulness.

I have decided to confess everything to Margot: my relapse, my happiness, and the name of the man I love. It won't be easy. Margot is not a woman to say: "I told you so!" but I feel pretty sure that I shall sadden and disappoint her, although she will not show it. "Burnt child though you are, you'll go back to the fire!" I am indeed going back to it, and with what joy!

I find Margot unchangeably true to herself in the big studio where she sleeps, eats and breeds her Brabançon dogs. Tall and upright, in her Russian blouse and long black jacket, she bends her pale face, with its lean cheeks framed in her rough grey bobbed hair, over a basket in which a minute dog in a flannel shirt, a little yellow monster, is groping about and gazing up at her with the beautiful, imploring eyes of a squirrel, under the bumpy forehead of a bonze. Round me yap and wriggle six cheeky little creatures whom a crack of a whip sends scampering to their straw kennels.

"What, Margot, another Brabançon? It's a passion!"

"Lord, no!" says Margot, sitting down opposite me and cradling the sick animal on her knees. "I don't love this poor little wretch."

"Someone gave her to you?"

"No, I bought her, of course. That will teach me not to walk in future past that old blackguard of a Hartmann, the dog-dealer. If you'd seen this Brabançon in the window, with her little face like a sick rat's and this spine protruding like a rosary, and above all those eyes. . . . Hardly anything touches me now, you know, except the expression of a dog for sale. So I bought her. She's half dead with enteritis; that never shows at the dealer's; they dope them with cacodylate. . . . Well now, my child, it's a long time since I saw you; are you working?"

"Yes Margot, I'm rehearsing."

"I can see that, you're tired."

With that familiar gesture of hers, she takes hold of my chin to tilt my face up and draw it towards her. Embarrassed, I close my eyes.

"Yes, you're tired. You've got older," she says in a very grave tone.

"Older! Oh, Margot!"

In that cry of pain and the flood of tears that follows it, my whole secret leaks out. I bury myself against my stern friend, and she strokes my shoulder and comforts me with the same "Poor little one!" that she used a moment ago to the sick Brabançon.

"There, there now, poor little one, there, there. It'll soon be all right. Look, here's some boracic lotion to bathe your eyes, I'd just prepared it for Mirette's. Not with your handkerchief! Take some cotton-wool . . . there! Poor little one, so your beauty's very necessary to you at present, is it?"

"Oh yes! . . . Oh Margot!"

" 'Oh, Margot!' Anyone might think I'd beaten you. Look at me. Are you very sore with me, poor little one?"

"No, Margot."

"You know very well," she goes on in her gentle, level voice, "that you can always count on finding here every kind of help, even the kind that hurts most: the truth. What was it I said to you? I said, you've got older."

"Yes . . . Oh, Margot . . ."

"Now don't begin again! But you've got older *this week*. You've got older *today*. Tomorrow, or in an hour's time, you'll be five years younger, ten years younger. If you'd come yesterday, or tomorrow, no doubt I should have said: 'My word, you've got younger!' "

126

"Just think, Margot, I shall soon be thirty-four."

"Don't expect me to pity you, I'm fifty-two!"

"It isn't the same thing, Margot, it's so important for me to be pretty, and young, and happy. I've . . . I . . ."

"You've got a lover?"

Her voice is still gentle, but the expression of her face has changed slightly.

"I haven't got a lover, Margot. Only, it's certain that I . . . I shall have one. But . . . I love him, you see!"

This kind of silly excuse amuses Margot.

"Ah, you love him? And he, too, loves you?"

"Oh!"

With a proud gesture, I protect my friend from the least suspicion.

"That's good. And . . . how old is he?"

"Just my age, Margot: very nearly thirty-four."

"That's . . . that's good."

I can't find anything else to add. I am horribly ill at ease. I had hoped, once the first embarrassment was over, to chatter about my happiness, and to tell everything about my friend, the colour of his eyes, the shape of his hands, his goodness, his honesty.

"He's . . . he's very nice, you know, Margot," I risked, shyly.

"So much the better, my child. You've made some plans, the two of you?"

"Plans? No . . . we haven't yet thought of anything. There's time."

"Yes of course, there's plenty of time. And what's happening about your tour, with all this?"

"My tour? Oh, this makes no difference to that."

"You're taking your . . . your fellow with you?"

Bathed in tears though I am, I can't help laughing when Margot refers to my friend with such squeamish discretion, as if she were speaking of something dirty.

"Taking him along, taking him . . . well . . . as a matter of fact, Margot, I don't at all know. I'll see."

My sister-in-law raises her eyebrows.

"You don't at all know, you have no plans, you'll see! My word, what an astonishing pair you are! What can you be thinking about? After all, it's the only thing you've got to do, to plan and prepare your future."

"The future. . . . Oh, Margot, I don't like preparing the future. It prepares itself without any help, and it comes so soon!"

"Is it a question of marriage or living in sin?"

I do not answer all at once, embarrassed for the first time by the chaste Margot's rather crude vocabulary.

"It isn't a question of anything. We're getting to know each other, finding out what we're like. . . ."

"You're finding out what you're like!"

With her mouth pursed and a cruel gaiety in her bright little eyes, Margot observes me.

"You're finding out what you're like! I see, you're at the stage when you're showing off to each other, is that it?"

"I assure you, Margot, we hardly show off at all," I say, forcing myself to smile. "That game's well enough for very young lovers, but he and I are no longer very young lovers."

"All the more reason," answers Margot, pitilessly. "You have more things to hide from each other. My little one," she added gently, "you know well enough you must laugh at my mania. Marriage seems to me such a monstrous thing. Haven't I often enough made you laugh by telling you how, from the very first days of my married life, I refused to share a bedroom with my husband because I thought it immoral to live at such close quarters with a young man who was a stranger to my family? I was born that way, that's the trouble, and I shall never change. . . . You haven't brought Fossette to see me today?"

Like Margot, I make an effort to cheer up.

"No, Margot. Your pack gave her such a poor welcome last time!"

"That's true. My pack isn't in very good shape at present. Come along, cripples!"

They do not have to be asked twice. From a row of kennels there emerge half a dozen dogs, a shivering, miserable little bunch, the biggest of which could be held in the crown of a hat. Saved by Margot from the "dog-dealer", wrested from that stupid, noxious trade which pens together in a window creatures that are sick, fattened up, starving or doped, I know nearly all of these. A few of them have become again, in her house, healthy, gay, robust animals; but others never get rid of their upset stomachs, their scabby skins, and their ineradicable hysteria. Margot looks after them as well as she can, discouraged by the thought that her charity is all to no purpose and that there will everlastingly be "luxury dogs" for sale.

The sick bitch has gone to sleep. I can find nothing to say. I look at the big room which, with its uncurtained windows, always has somewhat the appearance of an infirmary. On a table there are rows of chemists' bottles, rolled bandages, a diminutive thermometer, a tiny little rubber pear for dogs' enemas. The room smells of iodine and Jeyes fluid. I suddenly feel I must go away, I must find again without an instant's delay my warm narrow room, with the hollowed divan, and the flowers, and the friend I love.

"Goodbye, Margot, I'm going."

"Off you go then, my child."

"You're not too cross with me?"

"What about?"

"For being so foolish, and ridiculous, for being in love, I mean. I had so sworn to myself . . ."

"Cross with you? My poor little one, that would be too unkind. A new love . . . you mustn't feel uncomfortable. Poor little one!"

I am in a hurry to get home. I feel frozen, shrunken, and so

129

sad. Never mind, it's done, what a relief! I've told Margot everything. I have received the cold douche I expected and I run to shake it off, to dry myself and expand in the warmth again. I lower my veil to hide the traces of my upset, and I run —run to him!

t e n

"MONSIEUR MAXIME IS HERE, WAITING FOR MADAME."
My charwoman Blandine now says "Monsieur
Maxime" in a tender tone, as if she were speaking
of her foster-child.

He is here!

I rush to my room and shut myself in: he mustn't see my
face! Quick! Rice-powder, kohl, lip-stick. . . . Oh dear, look
at that shiny groove under my eye, still moist from my tears!
"You've got older." Silly thing, to go and cry like a little girl!
Haven't you learnt to suffer "dry-eyed"? Where are the days
when my glistening tears rolled down the velvet of my cheeks
without wetting it? There was a time when, to conquer my
husband all over again, I knew how to adorn myself with my
tears, weeping with my face lifted towards him and my eyes
wide open, and shaking but not drying the slow pearls which
made me more beautiful. How poor I have become!

"There you are at last, my darling, my scented one, my
appetising one, my . . ."

"Goodness, how silly you are!"

"Thank Heaven, yes!" sighs my friend in a tone of blissful
conviction.

He begins to indulge in his favourite game of lifting me up
in his arms till I touch the ceiling, and then kissing my cheeks,
chin, ears and mouth. I resist enough to force him to show his
strength, but he gets the upper hand in the struggle and then

he tips me right over on his arm, head down and feet in air until I cry "Help!", when he sets me upright again. The dog rushes to my defence and mingles her hoarse barks with our laughter and cries, in this rough game which I much enjoy.

What a good thing this healthy silliness is! And what a gay companion I have in him, as little concerned to appear clever as to avoid rumpling his tie. How warm it is here, and how quickly our laughter changes from the laughter of two opponents, confronting each other, to a voluptuous challenge. He devours his "appetising one", tasting her slowly, like a gourmet.

"How good you would be to eat, my darling. Your mouth is honeyed, but your arms, when I bite them, are salty, just a tiny bit, and so are your shoulders and knees. I feel sure you're salty from head to foot, like a cool shell, aren't you?"

"You'll know that only too soon, Big-Noodle!"

For I still call him "Big-Noodle", but . . . in a different tone.

"When? This evening? It's Thursday today, isn't it?"

"I think so . . . yes . . . why?"

"Thursday . . . that's a very good day."

Lying back among the cushions, and very happy, he says foolish things. A lock of his hair has fallen over his eyes, which have the vague look that a great wave of desire gives them, and he half opens his mouth to breathe. Whenever he adopts an abandoned attitude, he turns again into a handsome country lad, a woodcutter "taking a nap" on the grass—not that I dislike that!

"Get up, Max; we must talk seriously."

"I don't want to be hurt!" he sighs plaintively.

"Really, Max!"

"No! I know what talking seriously means. Mother always calls it that when she wants to speak of business, or money-matters, or marriage."

He snuggles into the cushions and closes his eyes. It is not the first time that he has shown that determination to be frivolous.

"Max, you've not forgotten that I'm going away on the fifth of April?"

He half opens his eyelids with their feminine lashes, and favours me with a long look.

"You're going away, darling? Whoever decided that?"

"Salomon, the impresario, and I."

"Good. But I haven't yet given my consent. Well, so be it then, you're going away. But if so, you're going away with me."

"With you!" I say, alarmed. "Don't you know what a tour is, then?"

"Of course I do. It's a journey . . . with me."

"With you?" I repeat. "For forty-five days! But haven't you anything to do, then?"

"Certainly I have. Since I've known you, I haven't a minute to myself, Renée."

That is prettily answered, but . . .

I gaze, disconcerted, at this man who has nothing to do, who always finds money in his pocket. He has nothing to do, that is a fact, I had never thought about it. He has no profession and no sinecure behind which to conceal his lazy freedom. How strange that is! Till I met him I never knew an idle man. He can give himself up entirely, day and night, to love, like . . . like a prostitute.

This quaint idea that, of the two of us, it is he who is the courtesan, causes me a sudden gaiety, and he quickly draws his touchy eyebrows together in a frown.

"What's the matter? Are you laughing? You shan't go!"

"I like that! And what about my forfeit?"

"I'll pay it."

"And Brague's forfeit? And the Old Troglodyte's?"

"I'll pay them."

Even if it is a joke, I do not altogether like it. Can I any longer doubt that we love each other? Here we are on the verge of our first quarrel.

I was mistaken, for here is my friend close to me, almost at my feet.

"My Renée, you shall do whatever you want, you know that."

But he has laid his hand on my forehead, and his eyes are fixed on mine, to read obedience there. Whatever I want? Alas! for the moment all I want is him.

"Is it still *The Pursuit* that you're taking on tour?"

"We're taking *The Dryad* too. Oh, what a lovely violet tie you have! It makes you look quite yellow."

"Leave my tie alone! *The Pursuit*, and *The Dryad*, and everything else, is an excuse to show your beautiful legs, and the rest."

"It's not for you to complain. Wasn't it on the boards that the 'rest' had the honour of being introduced to you?"

He presses me to him until it hurts.

"Be quiet! I remember. Every evening for five days I said hurting things to myself, final things every time. I thought I was a fool to go to the *Emp'-Clich'* as you call it, and when your act was over I would leave, calling myself every kind of name. And then next day I would weakly compromise: 'This truly is the last evening I shall be seen at that dump! But I just want to make sure what colour Renée Néré's eyes are. And besides, yesterday I didn't manage to arrive for the beginning.' In short, I was idiotic already."

"Idiotic already! You have a gift for putting things attractively, Max. It seems so queer to me that anyone can fall in love with a woman merely by looking at her."

134

"That depends on the woman one looks at. You know nothing about these things, Renée Néré. Just imagine, after I'd seen you mime *The Pursuit* for the first time, I spent at least an hour trying to sketch a diagram of your face. I succeeded, and I repeated I don't know how many times, in the margins of a book, a little geometric design that conveyed something to me alone. There was also, in your mime, a moment that filled me with unbearable joy: the moment when you sat on the table and read the threatening letter from the man you were deceiving. D'you know? You slapped your thigh, throwing back your head to laugh, and one could hear that your thigh was bare under your thin dress. The gesture was so robust you might have been a young fishwife, but your face glowed with a wonderfully sharp, refined wickedness, worlds apart from your accessible body. D'you remember?"

"Yes, yes . . . like this. Brague was pleased with me in that scene. But that, Max, is . . . is admiration, desire! Has it changed into love since then?"

"Changed?" He looked at me, very surprised. "I've never thought about it. I expect I loved you from that very moment. There are lots of women more beautiful than you, but . . ."

With a gesture of his hand he expresses all that is incomprehensible and irremediable in love. . . .

"But Max, what if, instead of a nice little bourgeoise like me, you'd chanced on a cold and calculating shrew, as tormenting as the itch! What then? Didn't the fear of that hold you back?"

"It never occurred to me," he said, laughing. "What a comic idea! When you love you don't think of so many things, you know."

He sometimes makes remarks like that which I, who think of so many things, feel as a rebuke.

"Little one," he murmurs, "why do you go in for this *café-concert* business?"

"Big-Noodle, why don't you go in for cabinet-making? Don't answer that you have the means to live otherwise, I know you have. But as for me, what would you have me do? Sewing, or typing, or street-walking? The music-hall is the job of those who never learnt one."

"But . . ."

I can hear from his voice that he is going to say something serious and embarrassing. I raise my head, which was resting on his shoulder, and gaze attentively at that face with its straight, firm nose, its fierce eyebrows sheltering the tender eyes, and the thick moustache under which hides a mouth with experienced lips.

"But, darling, you no longer need the music-hall now that I am there, and that . . ."

"Shh!"

Agitated and almost terrified, I urge him to stop. Yes, he is there, and ready for every kind of generosity. But that doesn't concern me, I don't want it to concern me. I cannot see that the fact that my friend is rich has anything to do with me. I cannot manage to fit him in to my future in the way he would like. No doubt that will come. I shall get used to the idea. I ask nothing better than to mingle my mouth with his and feel in advance that I belong to him, yet I can't associate his life with mine. If he were to announce to me: "I'm getting married," I feel I should answer politely: "All my congratulations!", thinking in my heart: "That doesn't concern me." And yet I wasn't exactly pleased, a fortnight ago, that he should eye little Jadin with such attention.

All these sentimental complications, fusses, hair-splittings, and psychological soliloquies, goodness how absurd I am! Would it not at bottom be more honest, and more worthy of a woman in love, to answer him: "Yes indeed you're there, and since we love each other, I'll ask you for everything. It's so simple. If I truly love you, you owe me everything, and any bread which does not come to me from you is impure."

What I have just thought is the right way to look at it. I ought to say it out loud, instead of remaining wheedlingly silent, rubbing my cheek against his shaven cheek, which has the smoothness of a very smooth piece of pumice-stone.

eleven

M Y OLD HAMOND HAD PERSISTED FOR SO MANY DAYS IN remaining at home, pleading rheumatism, influenza, or urgent work, that I ordered him to come at once. He delayed no longer and, when he came, his discreet and casual air, like that of a relation visiting some newly-weds, doubled my joy at seeing him again.

So here we are again, in affectionate tête-à-tête, like the old days.

"Like the old days, Hamond. Yet what a change!"

"Thank goodness, my child. Are you at last going to be happy?"

"Happy?"

I look at him with genuine astonishment.

"No, I shan't be happy. I don't even think of it. Why should I be happy?"

Hamond clacks his tongue; that is his way of scolding me. He thinks I have an attack of neurasthenia.

"Oh, come now, Renée. Isn't it going as well as I thought, then?"

I burst out laughing, very gay.

"Yes, of course it's going well, Hamond, only too well. I'm afraid we're beginning to adore each other."

"Well then?"

"Well then! D'you think that's a reason why I should be happy?"

Hamond cannot help smiling, and now it is my turn to look on the gloomy side.

"What torments you've thrust me into all over again, Hamond! For you'll admit it was your doing. Torments," I added in a lower tone, "that I wouldn't exchange for the greatest joys."

"Well," bursts out Hamond, relieved, "at least you're saved from that past which was fermenting inside you. I'd really had enough of seeing you gloomy and defiant, entangled in your memory and fear of Taillandy. Forgive me, Renée, but I would have stooped to pretty low things to endow you with a new love."

"You would, would you! D'you think that a new love, as you call it, destroys the memory of the first or . . . resuscitates it?"

Disconcerted by the asperity of my question, Hamond does not know what to say. But he has touched my sore spot so clumsily! And besides, he is only a man: he does not understand. He must have loved so many times: he no longer understands. His consternation makes me relent.

"No, my friend, I'm not happy. I'm . . . better or worse than that. Only . . . I don't at all know where I'm going. I want to say that to you before I become Maxime's mistress completely."

"Or his wife!"

"His wife?"

"Why not?"

"Because I don't want to."

My quick answer flies ahead of my reasoning, like an animal jumping wide of the snare before it sees it.

"Anyway that's of no importance," says Hamond carelessly. "It's the same thing."

"You think it's the same thing? For you, perhaps, and for many men. But for me! D'you remember, Hamond, what marriage was for me? No, I'm not thinking of the betrayals, you mistake me. I'm thinking of conjugal domesticity, which turns so many wives into a sort of nurse for a grown-up. Being married means . . . how shall I put it? It means trembling lest Monsieur's cutlet should be overdone, his Vittel water not cold enough, his shirt badly starched, his stiff collar soft, or the bath too hot! It means playing the exhausting part of an intermediary buffer between Monsieur's ill humour, his avarice, his greed, his laziness . . ."

"You're forgetting lust, Renée," interrupts Hamond gently.

"No, I jolly well am not! The part of mediator, I tell you, between Monsieur and the rest of humanity. You can't know, Hamond, you've been so little married! Marriage means . . . means: 'Tie my tie for me! . . . Get rid of the maid! . . . Cut my toe-nails! . . . Get up and make me some camomile! . . . Prepare me an emetic. . . .' It means: 'Give me my new suit, and pack my suit-case so that I can hurry to join her!' Steward, sick-nurse, children's nurse—enough, enough, enough!"

I end by laughing at myself and at the long scandalised face of my old friend.

"Oh, for goodness' sake, Renée, if you knew how this mania of yours for generalising gets on my nerves! 'In this country all the servant-girls are red-haired.' One doesn't always marry Taillandy! And I give you my word that, for my humble part, I should have blushed to ask a woman one of those petty services which . . . very much the contrary!"

I clap my hands. "Oh fine, I'm going to learn everything! Very much the contrary: I'm sure there was no one to touch you at buttoning up boots or flattening the press-studs on a tailored skirt? Alas, everyone can't marry Hamond!"

After a silence, I go on in a tone of weariness: "Let me generalise, as you say, even though I've had only one experience, as a result of which I'm still feeling shattered. I'm no longer young enough, or enthusiastic enough, or generous enough to go in for marriage again, or married life, if you prefer. Let me stay alone in my closed bedroom, bedecked and idle, waiting for the man who has chosen me to be his harem. I want to know nothing of him but his tenderness and his ardour, I want nothing from love, in short, but love."

"I know a good many people," says Hamond after a silence, "who would call that kind of love libertinism."

I shrug my shoulders, vexed at having made myself so little understood.

"Yes," insists Hamond, "libertinism. But since I know you . . . a little, I'd rather suppose that there is in you a fanciful, childish longing for the unrealisable: the loving couple, imprisoned in a warm room, isolated by four walls from the rest of the world—the normal dream of any young girl very ignorant of life."

"Or of a woman already mature, Hamond."

He protests, with a polite, evasive gesture, and avoids a direct answer.

"In any case, my dear child, it is not love."

"Why?"

My old friend throws away his cigarette almost angrily.

"Because! You said to me just now: 'Marriage for a woman means accepting a painful and humiliating domesticity; it means *tie my tie, prepare me an emetic, keep an eye on my cutlet, put up with my bad temper and my betrayals.*' You ought to have said *love* and not *marriage*. For only love makes the bond-service you speak of easy and joyful and glorious. You hate it at present, you repudiate it and spew it from you, because you no longer love Taillandy. But remember the time when, in the name of love, the tie, the footbath and the camomile tea became sacred symbols, revered and terrible. Remember the miserable part you played! I used to shake with indignation at seeing you being used almost like a go-between, aiding and abetting Taillandy and his women friends, but when one day I lost all discretion and all patience, you answered me: 'To love is to obey.' Be frank, Renée, be clear-sighted, and tell me whether all your sacrifices haven't only lost their value in your eyes since you recovered your free will? You assess them at their true worth *now that you no longer love.* Before—I've seen you at it, I know you, Renée—did you not unconsciously enjoy the merciful numbness which love dispenses?"

What is the good of answering? Nevertheless I am ready to argue, with all the unfairness in the world: the only thing that could rouse my pity today is this poor man who lists my conjugal misfortunes while thinking of his own. How young and "hurtable" he is, and quite saturated with the poison he longed to get rid of! We've moved a long way from my adventure and from Maxime Dufferein-Chautel.

I wanted to confide in Hamond and ask his advice. What is it that always leads us, scratched all over with dead thorns, invincibly back to the past? I have the feeling that, if Maxime came in, Hamond and I would not have time enough to change those faces of ours that no one ought to see: Hamond is all yellow with bile, with a little nervous tic in his left cheek, and as for me, my brows are knitted as if in the throes of a migraine, and my neck is thrust tensely forward, that strong neck that is beginning to lose the smooth suppleness of its youthful flesh.

"Hamond," I say very gently, "to change the subject, you aren't forgetting that I have to go off on tour?"

"To go off. . . . Yes, of course," he says, like a man being wakened from sleep. "What of it?"

"What of it! What about Maxime?"

"You're taking him, naturally?"

" 'Naturally!' It's not as simple as you seem to think. Life on tour is terrible . . . for a couple. There are the awakenings and departures in the early hours or the middle of the night, and interminable evenings for the one who waits, and then the hotel! What a beginning for a honeymoon! Even a woman of twenty wouldn't dare to risk being surprised at dawn, or sleeping in the train, that sleep that comes at the end of exhausting days, when one looks like a slightly swollen corpse. No, no, that's too great a danger for me. And besides, he and I deserve better than that. I'd vaguely thought of postponing our . . ."

"Heart-to-heart . . ."

"Thank you . . . until the end of the tour, and then to begin a life, oh! such a life! Not to think any more, Hamond, to go to ground somewhere, with him, in a country where, within reach of my mouth and my hands, I should find everything that offers itself and then escapes from me on the other side of the train window: moist leaves, flowers nodding in the wind, fruits with the bloom on their skins, and above all, streams of free, wayward, living water. You know, Hamond, when you've been living in a train for thirty days, you can't think how the sight of running water, between banks of new grass, parches your whole skin with a kind of indefinable thirst. During my last tour, I remember, we used to travel all morning and often all afternoon too. At noon, the farm girls would be milking the cows in the fields: I could see, in the deep grass, pails of burnished copper where the foaming milk squirted in thin straight jets. What a thirst, what an agonised longing I used to feel for that warm milk, topped with foam. It was a real little daily torture, I assure you. That is why I want to enjoy, all at the same time, everything I lack: pure air, a generous country where everything is to be found, and my love."

Involuntarily, I stretch out my arms, with my hands clasped, in the effort to invoke all I desire. Hamond goes on listening as though I had not stopped speaking.

"And then, my child, afterwards?"

"What d'you mean, 'afterwards'?" I say vehemently. "Afterwards? But that's all. I don't ask for anything more."

"That's fortunate," he murmurs to himself. "I mean, how will you live after, with Maxime? You'll give up your tours? You won't . . . work any longer in the music-hall?"

This question of his, so natural, is enough to bring me up short, and I look at my old friend defiantly, anxiously, almost intimidated:

"Why shouldn't I?" I say, feebly.

He shrugs his shoulders.

"Come now, Renée, think for a moment. Thanks to

Maxime you can live comfortably, even luxuriously, and take up again, as we all hope, that witty pen which is growing rusty. And then perhaps a child; what a fine little chap he would be!"

Rash Hamond! Is he yielding to his impulse as an ex-genre painter? This little picture of my future life, between a faithful lover and a beautiful child, produces in me the most inexplicable and disastrous effect. And he elaborates it, the poor wretch. He labours the point, without noticing the horrid gaiety dancing in my eyes which avoid his, and that the only replies he is getting from me are an occasional bored "yes", and the "I don't know, I suppose so", of a schoolgirl who is finding the lesson too long.

t w e l v e

A BEAUTIFUL CHILD; A FAITHFUL HUSBAND; AFTER ALL THERE was nothing to laugh at in that. I am still wondering what was the reason for my cruel hilarity. A beautiful child; I confess that I have never thought of it. When I was married I had not the time, being occupied first with love and then with jealousy, monopolised, in a word, by Taillandy, who in any case was not at all anxious to encumber himself with an expensive progeny.

So here am I, having spent thirty-three years without ever considering the possibility of being a mother. Am I a monster? A beautiful child: grey eyes, a sharp little nose, and the look of a little fox, like his mother, big hands and broad shoulders, like Maxime. It's no good; no matter how much I try I can't *see* him and I don't love him, the child I might have had, that I perhaps shall have.

"Tell me, what d'you feel about it, darling Big-Noodle?"

He has just come in, very quietly, already so much a part of my mind that I go on with my soul-searching in his presence.

"What d'you feel about the child we might have? It's Hamond who wants one, would you believe it!"

My friend opens enormous eyes and a round, astonished Pierrot mouth, and cries: "Long live Hamond! He shall have his kid, right away if you like, Renée."

I defend myself, for he goes for me with a mixture of roughness and passion, biting a little and kissing a lot, with that famished air which makes me feel just pleasantly frightened.

"A child!" he cries, "a little one of our own! I'd never thought of it, Renée. How intelligent Hamond is! It's a brilliant idea."

"D'you think so, my darling? Selfish brute that you are! It doesn't matter a scrap to you that I should be deformed and ugly, and that I should suffer, does it?"

He laughs again and pins me down on the divan at arms' length.

"Deformed? Ugly? What a goose you are, Madame! You'll be magnificent, and so will the little one too, and it will all be the greatest fun."

Then all at once he stops laughing and draws his fierce eyebrows together above his gentle eyes.

"And then, at least, you'd never be able to leave me and go gadding about the world all alone, would you? You'd be caught."

Caught. I give in, and play lazily with the fingers which hold me. But giving in is also a ruse of the weak. Caught. He did indeed say that, in a transport of egoism. I summed him up correctly, the time when I laughingly called him a monogamous bourgeois, and a home-loving paterfamilias.

So I might end my days, peacefully, dwarfed by his large shadow? Would his faithful eyes still love me when my graces had faded one by one? Ah, what a difference, what a difference from *the other*! Except that *the other* also spoke as a master and knew how to say under his breath, as he gripped me with a rough grasp: "Keep your head up and walk on, I'm holding you!" How I suffer! Their differences hurt me and so do their resemblances. And I stroke the forehead of this one, so unaware and innocent, and call him "my little one".

145

"Don't call me your 'little one', darling, it makes me ridiculous."

"I'll make you ridiculous if I want to. You are my little one because you're younger than . . . than your age, because you've suffered very little, and loved very little, because you aren't cruel. . . . Listen to me, my little one: I'm going away."

"Not without me, Renée!"

How he cried out! It makes me shiver with pain and pleasure.

"Without you, my darling, without you. I must. Listen to me. No . . . Max . . . I shall speak all the same, after . . . Listen Max. D'you mean you don't want to, you can't, wait for me? Don't you love me enough then?"

He tears himself from my hands and draws violently away from me.

"Not enough, not enough! Oh, these womanish reasonings! I don't love you enough if I follow you, and not enough if I stay. Admit it: if I'd answered you: 'Very well, darling, I'll wait for you,' what would you have thought of me? And you, who go away when you could quite well not go away, how d'you expect me to believe that you love me? After all . . ."

He plants himself in front of me, head thrust forward and suddenly suspicious: "After all, you've never said it to me."

"Said what?"

"That you love me."

I feel myself blushing as if he had caught me out in something.

"You've never said it to me," he repeats obstinately.

"Oh Max!"

"You've said to me . . . you've said to me: 'Darling . . . my beloved Big-Noodle . . . Max . . . my darling love,' and you groaned aloud, as though you were singing, the day when . . ."

"Max!"

"Yes, that day when you couldn't prevent yourself from calling me 'My love', but you've never said to me: 'I love you.'"

It is true. I had desperately hoped that he would not notice it. One day, another lovely day, I sighed so loudly in his arms that the words "love you" breathed from me like a slightly louder sigh, and all at once I became silent and cold.

"Love you." I don't want to say it again, never again. I never want to hear again that voice, my voice of other days, broken and low, irresistibly murmuring that word of long ago. Only, I know no other that will do. There is no other.

"Tell me, tell me that you love me. Tell me, I implore you."

My lover has knelt down before me and his imperious prayer will give me no peace. I smile in his face, as if I were resisting him for fun, and all of a sudden I want to hurt him so that he may suffer a little too. But he is so gentle, so far away from my suffering. Why should I hold him responsible for it? He doesn't deserve that.

"Poor darling, don't be naughty, don't be sad. Yes, I love you, I love you, oh, I do love you. But I don't want to say it to you. I'm so proud at heart, if you only knew."

Leaning against my breast, he closes his eyes, accepts my lie with a fond assurance, and goes on hearing me say "I love you" when I have ceased to speak.

What a strange burden he seems to these arms that have been empty for so long! I don't know how to rock so big a child, and how heavy his head is! But let him rest there, sure of me. Sure of me because he is a prey to a time-honoured delusion which makes him jealous of my present and my roving future, but lets him rest trustfully against this heart that another inhabited for so long. Rash and honest lover that he is, it does not occur to him that he shares me with a memory, and that he will never taste that best of all glories, the glory of being able to say to me: "I bring you a joy and a sorrow that you have never known."

147

There he is, on my breast. Why he, and not another? I don't know. I gaze down at his brow, I feel I want to protect him against myself, to excuse myself for giving him only a heart that has been deconsecrated, if not cleansed. I would like to safeguard him against the harm I can do him. Well, there it is as Margot foretold: I'm going back to the fire. But a reliable fire this time, with nothing infernal about it; in fact much more like a family kettle.

"Wake up, darling."

"I'm not asleep," he murmurs, without lifting his beautiful lashes. "I'm breathing you in."

"You'll wait for me in Paris, while I'm on tour? Or will you go to your mother's in the Ardennes?"

He gets up without answering and smooths his hair with the flat of his hand.

"Well?"

He takes his hat from the table and turns to go with lowered eyes, still silent. With a bound I am on him, clinging to his shoulders: "Don't go away, don't go away! I'll do whatever you want, come back, don't leave me alone, oh, don't leave me alone!"

Whatever has happened to me? I've suddenly become nothing but a poor wisp of a thing, drenched with tears. It seemed to me that if he went away, with him would go warmth and light and that second love all mingled with the burning ashes of the first, but so dear, so unhoped for. I cling to my lover with the hands of a drowning person, and stammer over and over again without hearing it: "Everyone leaves me, I'm all alone."

Loving me as he does, he well knows that there is no need of words or reasonings to calm me, but only cradling arms, a warm murmur of vague caressing words, and kisses, endless kisses.

"Don't look at me, my darling, I'm ugly, my eye-black has got rubbed off and my nose is red. I'm ashamed to have been so foolish."

148

"My Renée, my little, little one, what a brute I've been. Yes, yes, I'm just a big brute. You want me to wait for you in Paris? I will. You want me to go to mother's? I'll go to mother's."

Undecided, and embarrassed by my victory, I no longer know what I want.

"Listen, Max darling, this is what we must do. I shall go

away, alone, about as eagerly as a whipped dog. We'll write to each other every day. And we'll put up with it heroically, won't we, so as to get to the date, the beautiful fifteenth of May, which will reunite us?"

The hero agrees sadly, with a resigned nod.

"The fifteenth of May, Max! I feel," say I in a lower voice, "that that day I shall throw myself into your arms as I would throw myself into the sea, as freely and as irremediably."

He replies to this with a look and an embrace which make me lose my head a little.

"And then, listen. If we can't wait, well never mind, you'll come and join me, I'll send for you. Now are you happy? After all, it's silly to be heroic and life's so short. That's fixed then. Whoever is the unhappier will join the other, or write to the other to come. But we'll still try, because a honeymoon in the train . . . Is it all right now? What are you looking for?"

"I'm thirsty, can you believe it, absolutely dying of thirst. Would you mind ringing for Blandine?"

"No need for her. You stay there and I'll go and get the things."

Happy and passive, he lets himself be waited on, and I watch him drinking as though he were granting me a great favour. If he wants me to, I'll tie his tie and decide what we'll have for dinner. And I'll bring him his slippers. And he shall ask me: "Where are you going?" as though he were my master. A female I was and, for better or worse, a female I find myself to be.

Relying on the dusk to hide my face whose ravages I have hastily restored, I sit on his knee and let him drink from my lips the breath that is still uneven from my sobs of a moment ago. One of his hands slides down from my forehead to my breast and I kiss it as it passes. Held in his arms, I fall back again into the state of a cherished victim who protests feebly against something she would not prevent if she could.

But all of a sudden I spring to my feet, struggle with him for a few seconds without saying a word, and finally manage to free myself crying "No!"

I had very nearly let myself be taken by surprise, there on that corner of the divan, his attempt was so swift and so clever. Out of reach, I look at him without anger and merely reproach him with: "Why did you do that? That was very naughty, Max."

Obedient and repentant, he sidles towards me, knocking over a little table and some chairs on his way, and murmuring "Forgive me . . . won't do it again . . . darling, it's so hard to wait . . ." in a somewhat exaggerated tone of childish supplication.

It is nearly dark now and I can no longer make out his features clearly. But I suspected that the suddenness of that attempt a moment ago was due as much to calculation as loss of control. "You would have been caught, and then you would no longer have gone off wandering about the world all on your own."

"Poor Max," I say to him, gently.

"Are you laughing at me? Have I been silly?" He humbles himself nicely, and cleverly. He wants to bring my thoughts back to the gesture itself, and so to prevent me from thinking of his true motives. And I lie a tiny bit, to reassure him.

"I'm not laughing at you, Max. There are precious few men, you know, who would risk losing all their prestige by throwing themselves on a woman as you did, you great idiot. It's your clumsy peasant air which saves you, and those eyes, like an amorous wolf's. You looked like a day labourer tumbling a girl by the roadside on his way home from work at nightfall."

I leave him, to go and encircle my eyes again with the blue outline which makes them velvety and shining, to put on a coat and to pin on my head one of those bell-shaped hats whose form and whose colours remind Max of Champfleury's "Animated Flowers", those little flower-fairies who wear on their heads a poppy inside-out, the cup of a lily-of-the-valley, or a big iris with drooping petals.

We go off together for a gentle drive in the motor in the darkness of the Bois. These evening promenades are dear to me, when I hold my love's hand in the dim light, to know that he is there and for him to know that I am there. Then I can close my eyes and dream that I am going away with him to an unknown country where I shall have no past and no name, and where I shall be born again with a new face and an untried heart.

thirteen

ONE WEEK MORE AND I LEAVE.

Shall I really leave? There are hours and days when I doubt it. Especially days of premature spring, when my love takes me to those parks outside Paris, flattened and rutted with motors and bicycles, yet made mysterious all the same by the sharp, fresh season. Towards the end of the afternoon, a mauve mist veils the avenues so that you do not know where they end, and the unexpected discovery of a wild hyacinth, with its three slender bells of artless blue swaying in the wind, has all the charm of a stolen joy.

On a sunny morning last week we went for a long walk in the Bois, where the grooms gallop their horses. Walking side by side, we felt energetic and happy but not very talkative, and I was humming a little song which makes you walk fast. At a bend in a deserted riding-track we stopped, nose to muzzle before a very young hind with a golden coat, who lost countenance at sight of us and stopped short instead of fleeing.

She was panting with emotion and her delicate knees trembled, but her long eyes, made longer still by a brown line—like mine—expressed more embarrassment than fear. I would have liked to touch her ears, which were pointed towards us and plushy like the leaves of mullein, and that soft velveteen muzzle. But when I stretched out my hand, she turned her forehead away timidly and disappeared.

"You wouldn't have killed her, out hunting, Max?"

"Kill a hind? Why not a woman?" he answered, simply.

That day we lunched at Ville-d'Avray, like everyone else, in that restaurant with the curious terraces, terraces for eating and sleeping, that overhang the edge of the water, and we were as sensible as lovers already surfeited with pleasure. I was glad to find that the open air and the pure wind and the trees inspired in Max the same exhilarating serenity with which they always fill me. I gazed at the smooth water of the pool, turbid water with patches of iridescence on its surface, and at the hazel bushes with their hanging catkins. Then my eyes returned to this good comrade who had come into my life, full of the firm hope that I might build for him a happiness that would endure as long as that life itself.

Shall I really leave? There are times when I busy myself, as if in a dream, with my departure. My sponge-bag, my rolled-up rug and my waterproof, unearthed from cupboards, have reappeared in the light of day, streaked and shapeless and looking as though they were worn out with travelling. Full of disgust, I turned out containers filled with rancid cold cream and yellowed vaseline stinking of paraffin.

For the time being I take no pleasure in handling these tools of my trade. And when Brague came round to see how I was getting on, I received him so absentmindedly and offhandedly that he departed in a huff and, much more serious, with a very polite "au revoir, dear friend". Never mind, there will be plenty of time to see him and smooth him out during those forty days. I am expecting him very soon now, to give me my final instructions. Max will come a little later.

"Good-morning, dear friend."

I thought as much; my comrade is still ruffled.

"No really, Brague, that's enough. That high-falutin' style doesn't suit you at all. We're here to talk business. You remind me of Dranem as the Sun-King when you call me 'dear friend'."

Quickly amused, Brague protests: "High-falutin' style indeed, and why not? I can outdo Castellane when I want to. Have you never seen me in a dress suit?"

"No."

"Neither have I. I say, it's dark in this little . . . boudoir of yours. Why don't we go into your bedroom? We could see better to talk."

"All right, let's go into my bedroom."

Brague immediately spots, on the mantelpiece, a photograph of Max: Max looking stiff in a new suit, the black of his hair too black, the white of his eyes too white, formal and slightly absurd but very handsome all the same.

Brague examines the portrait as he rolls his cigarette.

"Definitely your 'friend', this chap, isn't he?"

"It's . . . my friend, yes." And I simper, idiotically.

"He's smart, there's no denying it. You'd take him for someone in the government. What are you laughing at?"

"Nothing. Just the thought that he might be in the government. That's hardly his line."

Brague holds a match to his cigarette and watches me out of the corners of his eyes.

"Taking him with you?"

I shrug my shoulders: "No, of course not. I couldn't. How could you expect . . ."

"But I don't *expect*, that's just it," cried Brague, his equanimity restored. "I think that's very right of you, my girl. You wouldn't believe how many tours I've seen bitched up because Madame wouldn't leave Monsieur, or because Monsieur wanted to keep an eye on Madame. It's nothing but arguments, billings and cooings, quarrels, reconciliations when they simply can't get out of bed, or else they totter feebly about the stage with black-ringed eyes: in short, it ruins the whole thing. Give me a cheerful trip where we're all pals. You know how I've always said that love and work don't go together, and I've never changed my mind about that. Besides, after all, forty days isn't eternity; you write to each other and when it's over you meet and team up again. Has he got an office, your friend?"

"An office? No, he hasn't got an office."

"Well, does he . . . make motor-cars? I mean, he's got some sort of business?"

"No."

"He does nothing?"

"Nothing."

Brague lets out a whistle that might be interpreted in at least two ways.

"Absolutely nothing at all?"

"Nothing. That's to say, he owns some forests."

"It's staggering."

"What staggers you?"

"That anyone can live like that. No office. No factory. No rehearsals. No racing stables. Doesn't it seem comic to you?"

I look up at him with an embarrassed and slightly conspiratorial air. "Yes."

I cannot make any other answer. My friend's idleness, that mooning about like a schoolboy on perpetual holiday, often fills me with dismay and almost scandalises me.

"It would kill me," declares Brague, after a silence. "A matter of habit."

"No doubt."

"Now," says Brague, sitting down, "let's be brief and to the point. You've got everything you need?"

"Of course I have! My Dryad's costume, the new one, is a dream. Green as a little grasshopper and weighs less than a pound. The other's been done up and re-embroidered and cleaned, and you'd swear it was new: it can do another sixty shows without showing any signs of wear."

Brague purses his mouth.

"H'm . . . you sure? You ought to have managed to stump up a new rig for *The Pursuit*."

"That's right, and you'd have paid me for it, wouldn't you? And talking about *The Pursuit*, what about your embroidered buckskin breeches that have taken on the colour of all the boards that have covered them with polish, am I reproaching you with them?"

My comrade lifts a dogmatic hand: "Don't let's confuse things, if you don't mind. My breeches are magnificent. They've taken on a patina, a richness; they have the colour of fine earthenware. It would be a crime to replace them."

"You're just a skinflint," I tell him, shrugging my shoulders.

"And you're a harpy."

It does us a world of good to go for each other a bit, it refreshes us. We're both just sufficiently roused for the dispute to seem like a lively rehearsal.

"Break it up!" cried Brague. "The costume question is settled. Now for the baggage question."

"As if I needed you for that! This isn't exactly the first time we've been away together, you know. Are you going to teach me how to fold my chemises?"

From between eyelids wrinkled by his grimaces on the stage, Brague casts on me a crushing look.

"You poor thing. Lop-sided and ill-shapen brain, go on. Talk, natter away, rouse your bee and let it buzz. Am I going to teach you? As if I could teach you! Listen, and try to take it in: we have to pay for our excess baggage ourselves, don't we?"

"Shh!"

I sign to him to stop, agitated because I have heard two discreet rings on the bell in the antechamber. It is *he*, and Brague is still there. After all, they know each other.

"Come in, Max, come in. It's Brague. We're talking of the tour; it won't bore you?"

No, it does not bore him; but it embarrasses me a little. These music-hall matters are poor, precise, commercial things, which I want to keep separate from my love, my darling lazy love.

Brague, very nice when he wants to be, smiles at Max.

"You don't mind, sir? It's our professional mixture we're

stirring, and I pride myself on being an economical cook who wastes nothing and doesn't make a bit on the side."

"Oh, please go on," cries Max. "On the contrary, it will amuse me, since it's all new to me. I shall learn."

Liar. For a man who is being amused, he looks very bad-tempered and very sad.

"As I was saying," Brague begins, "on the last tour, the September one, if you remember we got through ten or eleven francs for excess baggage every day, as if we'd been Carnegie."

"Not all the time, Brague."

"No, not all the time. There were days when we paid three francs or four francs excess. Even that's too much. As far as I'm concerned, I've had enough of it. What have you got in the way of luggage, besides your suitcase?"

"My black trunk."

"The big one? It's madness. I won't have it."

Max coughs.

"This is what you'll do: you'll use mine. In the top-layer: stage costumes. Second compartment; our underthings, your chemises, your knickers and your stockings, my shirts, my pants, etcetera."

Max fidgets.

". . . and at the bottom, shoes, change of suit for you and me, oddments, etcetera. Understand?"

"Yes, not a bad idea."

"All the same . . ." says Max.

"Like that," goes on Brague, "we've got just one piece of big luggage (the Troglodyte'll manage somehow. His mother, who's a poultry plucker, will lend him a basket) *one*, in all and for all. That means no excess, and reduction of tips to station porters, stage hands, etcetera. If we don't each make five francs a day on that, I'm a Dutchman. You change your underwear every how often, on tour?"

I blush, because of Max.

"Every two days."

"That's your affair. We can get our washing done in the big

burgs, Lyons, etcetera. So I reckon twelve chemises and twelve little pantikins, and the rest in proportion; isn't that big and generous? In short, I rely on you to be reasonable."

"Don't worry."

Brague gets up and grasps Max's hand.

"You see it doesn't take long to button up, sir. As for you, rendezvous at the station, at quarter past seven on Tuesday morning."

I accompany him as far as the antechamber and, when I come back, a tempest of protestations, lamentations and reproaches greets me.

"Renée, it's monstrous, it isn't possible, you've lost your head. Your chemises, your own chemises, and your far-too-short little pantaloons, my darling love, hugger-mugger with the underdrawers of that individual. And your stockings with his socks, I dare say. How contemptible and how sordid!"

"How d'you mean, how sordid? It mounts up to two hundred francs."

"That's just what I mean, it's all so paltry."

I restrain a reply which would wound him: where could he, the spoilt child, have learnt that money, the money one earns, is a respectable, serious thing which one handles with care and speaks about solemnly?

He wipes his forehead with a beautiful handkerchief of violet silk. For some time past my friend has shown a great concern for elegance: he has magnificent shirts, handkerchiefs to match his ties, and shoes with doeskin spats. I have not failed to notice this for, on this dear Big-Noodle with his somewhat heavy build, the slightest detail of dress takes on an almost shocking importance.

158

"Why do you agree to it?" he asks me reproachfully. "It's odious, this promiscuity."

Promiscuity. I was expecting that word. It is widely used. The "promiscuity of the stage".

"Tell me, darling," I say, tapering the points of his silky, rusty-black moustache between two fingers, "if it were a question of *your* shirts and *your* underdrawers, that wouldn't be *promiscuity?* You must remember that I'm only a very sensible little *'caf'conc' '* who lives by her job."

He suddenly embraces me, crushing me a little on purpose.

"The devil take your job. Ah, when I have you all to myself, you'll see. I'll absolutely load you with first-class carriages, and racks full of flowers, and frocks and frocks, and every beautiful thing I can find and everything I can invent."

His beautiful sombre voice ennobles this commonplace promise. Beneath the words I can hear, vibrating in it, his desire to lay the whole universe at my feet.

Frocks? I realise he must find my tailored suits of grey, brown and dark blue very monotonous and severe, a kind of neutral crysalis which I exchange, once the footlights are lit, for painted gauzes, shining spangles, and iridescent swirling skirts. First-class carriages? What for? They don't go any further than the others.

Fossette has squeezed between us her monk-like skull, which gleams like rosewood. My little companion scents a departure. She has recognised the suitcase, with its rubbed corners, and the waterproof, she has seen the black-enamelled English tin box and the make-up case. She knows that I shall not take her, and resigns herself in advance to a life, petted it must be added, of rambles on the fortifications, evenings with the concierge, dinners in town and teas in the Bois. "I know you'll come back," say her slit eyes, "but when?"

"Max, she's very fond of you; you'll look after her?"

There now, the mere fact of bending together over this anxious little creature makes our tears overflow. I hold mine back with an effort which makes my throat and nose sting. How beautiful my love's eyes look, enlarged by the two lustrous tears which wet his eyelashes. Ah, why leave him?

"In a little while," he murmurs in a stifled voice, "I'll go and fetch a . . . beautiful little handbag . . . that I've ordered for you . . . very strong . . . for the journey. . . ."

"Oh, Max, have you?"

"In . . . pigskin. . . ."

"Max, come now, be a bit braver than I am."

He blows his nose, rebelliously.

"Why should I? I don't want to be brave, I don't. On the contrary."

"We're absurd. Neither would have dared to give way to our feelings on our own account, but Fossette has set us off. It's the trick of the 'little table' in *Manon*, and of the one-armed man in *Poliche*, d'you remember?"

Max dries his eyes, very slowly and carefully, with the simplicity with which he does everything, and which saves him from ridicule.

"I daresay you're right, my Renée. Anyway, if ever you want to turn me into a fountain, you need only talk to me of everything which surrounds you here in this little flat, everything that I shan't see again until you return. This old divan, the armchair where you sit to read, and your portraits, and the ray of sunshine gliding over the carpet from midday until two o'clock." He smiles, very moved. "Don't talk to me of the coal-shovel, of the hearth or the tongs or I shall break down!"

He has gone to get the beautiful little pigskin handbag.

"When we live together," he said to me wheedlingly, before he went out, "will you give me the furniture of this little sitting-room? I'll have some more made for you."

I smiled, to avoid refusing. These bits and pieces at Max's? For lack of money I have never replaced these relics of my conjugal home, which Taillandy let me take by way of contemptible compensation for the author's rights of which he formerly cheated me. What a "little table" aria I could sing about that would-be Dutch fumed oak, about that old divan worn into hollows by wanton games to which I was not bidden! Haunted furniture it is, amidst which I have often awakened with the mad fear that my liberty was only a dream. A strange wedding-present for a new lover. A shelter, and not a home, that is all I leave behind me: first- and second-class travelling boxes, hotels of every type, and sordid music-hall dressing-rooms in Paris and the provinces and abroad, have been more familiar and more benevolent to me than this place which my love calls "a charming, cosy nest".

How many times, in fleeing from myself, have I not fled from this ground floor? Today when, beloved and in love, I am leaving, I would like to be still more loved, still more loving, and so changed as to be unrecognisable in my own eyes. No doubt it is too soon, and the time has not yet come. But at least I am leaving with a troubled mind, overflowing with re-gret and hope, urged to return and reaching out towards my new lot with the glorious impulse of a serpent sloughing off its dead skin.

Part Three

one

"*GOODBYE, MY DEAR LOVE. My trunk is shut. My lovely pig-skin bag, my travelling costume, and the long veil to go over my hat are laid out on our big divan, looking sad and sensible and awaiting my awakening tomorrow. Out of reach of you and my own weakness, I feel I have left already, so I give myself the joy of writing you my first love-letter.*

"*You'll receive this express-letter tomorrow morning, just at the time when I'm leaving Paris. It's merely an au revoir, written before I sleep, to let you know that I love you so much, that you mean so much to me! I am desolate at leaving you.*

"*Don't forget that you've promised to write to me 'all the time', and to console Fossette. And on my side I promise to bring you back a Renée tired of touring, grown thinner with solitude, and freed from everything, except you.*

Your
Renée."

The swift shadow of a bridge passes rapidly over my eyelids which I was keeping closed, and I open them again to see, receding rapidly on the left of the train, that little field of potatoes that I know so well, huddled against the high wall of the fortifications.

I am alone in the compartment. Brague, severely economical, is travelling second with the Old Troglodyte. A wet day, languid as a grey dawn, lies heavy over the countryside with its trails of smoke from factories. It is eight o'clock and the first morning of my trip. After a short period of dejection, following the agitation of departure, I had fallen into a glum immobility which made me hope for sleep.

I pull myself together and proceed to make my preparations, mechanically, like an old campaigner: I unfold the camel-hair travelling-rug, blow up the two silk-covered rubber cushions—one for my back and one for the nape of my neck—and hide my hair under a veil of the same bronze colour. I do all that methodically and carefully, though a sudden indescribable anger makes my hands tremble the while. A real fury, yes, and against myself. I am leaving, each turn of the wheel carries me further from Paris, I am leaving, while an icy spring adorns the tips of the oak branches with frozen pearls; all is cold and damp, with a mist which smells of winter still, and I am leaving when I might at this hour be lying, relaxed with pleasure, against the warm side of a lover. I feel as though my anger were whetting in me a devouring appetite for all that is pleasant, luxurious, easy and selfish, a need to let myself slide down the softest slope, and embrace with arms and lips a belated happiness that is tangible and ordinary and delicious.

How tedious to me is everything that I see in this familiar suburb, with its pallid villas where the yawning housewives in their chemises rise late to shorten the empty days. I would have done better not to have left Brague, to have remained with him in the dirty, blue-cushioned seats of the second-class carriages, among the good-natured chatter, the human odour of the crowded compartment, and the smoke of cigarettes at sixpence the packet.

The ta-ta-tam of the train, which I hear in spite of myself, acts as an accompaniment to the dance motif of *The Dryad*, which I hum with the persistence of one possessed. How long will this impression of having dwindled last? For I feel myself diminished, and weakened, as though I had been bled. During my saddest days the sight of a quite ordinary landscape, as long as it was receding rapidly to right and left, and as long as it was veiled from time to time with a ribbon of smoke that got torn on the thorn hedges, acted all the same on me like a health-giving tonic. I am cold. A wretched morning sleep numbs me, and I feel as though I were fainting rather than sleeping, agitated by childish arithmetical dreams in which this wearisome question keeps recurring: "if you have left half of yourself behind, does that mean you have lost fifty per cent of your original value?"

t w o

Dijon, April 3rd.

"YES, YES, I'M WELL. Yes, I found your letter; yes, I'm having a success. Ah, my darling, know the whole truth. When I left you I sank into the most absurd, the most impatient despair. Why did I go away? Why did I leave you? Forty days! I shall never be able to bear that, now. And I'm only at the third town.

> At the third town
> Her lover puts on her
> A gown of gold and a silver gown.

"Alas, my lover, I need neither silver nor gold, but only you. It rained at my first two stopping-places, to make me realise better my hateful desertion, there between hotel walls papered with chocolate and beige, and in those imitation oak dining-rooms which the gas makes darker still.

"You don't know what discomfort is, you spoilt son of Madame Ever-Cut. When we're together again, just to rouse your indignation and make you cherish me still more, I'll tell you of the returns at midnight to the hotel, with the make-up box weighing heavily on my tired arm, the waiting at the door under the fine mist while the night-porter slowly wakes, the horrible room with its badly-dried sheets, the minute jug of hot water which has had time to get cold. And should I make you share these daily joys? No, my darling, let *me exhaust my own powers of resistance before I cry to you 'Come, I can't bear it another minute!'*

"Anyway, it's fine here at Dijon, and I welcome this sun timidly, like a present that's going to be quickly taken away from me.

"You promised me to console Fossette. She's yours as much as mine. Take care not to overwhelm her with attentions while I'm away, or she won't forgive you. Her bulldog sensibility is such as to impose on her an exquisite repression of her feelings, and when I desert her, she greatly resents it if some affectionate third person notices her grief, even by an attempt to distract her from it.

"Goodbye, goodbye, I kiss you and I love you. Such a cold twilight today, you can't imagine. The sky's as green and pure as it is in January when it's freezing hard. Write to me, love me, warm your
                                                                    Renée."

                                                                April 10th
"My last letter must have made you unhappy. I'm not pleased with myself, nor with you either. You have a beautiful writing, bold and round, and at the same time slender, elegant and curly, like the plant that in my part of the world we call 'flowering osier'; it fills four or even eight pages with loving maledictions and the most burning regrets and a few 'I adore you's'. It can be read in twenty seconds and I'm sure you genuinely think you've written me a long letter. Moreover, you talk of nothing but me in it.

"My darling, I've just passed through, without stopping, a region which belongs to me because I spent my childhood there. I felt as though a long caress were stroking my heart. One day, promise me, we'll go there together? No, no—what am I writing—we won't go there. In your memory your Ardennes forests would put to shame my coppices of oaks and brambles and white-beam, and you would not see, as I do, trembling above them and the shadowy waters of the springs, and above the blue hill adorned with the tall flowers of the thistle, the slender rainbow which magically enshrines all things in the place where I was born.

"Nothing has changed there. A few new roofs, bright red, that's all. Nothing has changed in my part of the world—except me. Ah,

169

my darling love, how old I am! Can you really love such an old young woman? I blush for myself, here. Why did you not know the tall child who used to trail her regal braids here, silent by nature as a wood nymph? All that, which once I was, I gave to another, to another than you! Forgive me for this cry, Max, it is the cry of my torment, which I've kept in ever since I loved you. And now that it's too late, are not the things you love in me the things which change me and deceive you, my curls clustering thick as leaves, my eyes which the blue kohl lengthens and suffuses, the artificial smoothness of my powdered skin? What would you say if I were to reappear, if I appeared before you with my heavy, straight hair, with my fair lashes cleansed of their mascara, in short with the eyes which my mother gave me, crowned with brief eyebrows quick to frown, grey, narrow, level eyes in the depths of which there shines a stern, swift glance which I recognise as that of my father?

"Don't be afraid, my darling love, I shall return to you more or less as I left you, a little more weary, a little more tender. Every time I touch the fringes of it, my own country casts a spell on me, filling me with sad, transitory rapture; but I would not dare to stop there. Perhaps it is only beautiful because I have lost it.

"Goodbye, dear, dear Max. We have to leave very early tomorrow, for Lyons, otherwise we shouldn't have our rehearsal with the orchestra, which I look after while Brague, never tired, sees to the programmes, the putting of our posters in the frames, and the sale of our postcards.

"Oh, how cold I was, last night again, in the flimsy dress I wear for The Pursuit. *Cold is my enemy, it paralyses my life and my thoughts. You know that, you in whose hands my own seek refuge, curled up like two leaves under the frost. I miss you, my dear warmth, as much as I miss the sun.*

*Your
Renée."*

three

O N WE GO. I EAT, SLEEP, WALK, MIME AND DANCE. NO ZEST,
but no effort. There is just one moment of excitement
in the whole day, the moment when I ask the porter
at the music-hall if there is "any post" for me. I read my
letters like one starved, leaning against the greasy door-post of
the artistes' entry, in the foetid draught that smells of cellars
and ammonia. But they make time hang more heavily afterwards, when there is no more left to read, when I have deci-
phered the date of the postmark and turned the envelope inside out as if I hoped to see a flower or a photo fall out of it.

I pay no attention to the towns where we play. I know them
and have no wish to explore them again. So I just tack on to
Brague, who goes about like a good-humoured conqueror taking possession once more of those familiar "little old burgs"—
Rheims, Nancy, Belfort and Besançon.

"That little coffee shop's still at the corner of the quay, did
you notice? I bet they recognise me when we go and dig in to
their sausage with white wine this evening."

He takes deep breaths, darts down the streets with the joy of
a vagabond, loiters round the shops, and climbs up to the
cathedrals. Last year it was I who led him, but now I accompany him. He trails me along in his shadow, and sometimes we
take the Old Troglodyte in tow too, though normally he goes
off alone, gaunt and seedy-looking in his thin jacket and over-
short trousers. Where does he sleep? Where does he eat? I

don't know. When I ask Brague he answered briefly: "Where he likes. I'm not his nurse."

The other evening, at Nancy, I caught sight of the Troglodyte in his dressing-room. He was standing there biting into a pound loaf and holding a slice of brawn delicately between two fingers. The sight of that poor man's meal, and the voracious movement of his jaws, made my heart contract and I went to find Brague.

"Brague, has the Troglodyte enough to live on on tour? He really does earn fifteen francs, doesn't he? Why doesn't he feed better?"

"He's saving," answers Brague. "*Everyone* saves on tour. *Everyone* isn't Vanderbilt or Renée Néré, to treat themselves to rooms at five francs and *café-au-laits* served in their rooms. The Troglodyte owes me for his costume, which I advanced him; he pays me for it at the rate of five francs a day. In twenty days he'll be able to guzzle oysters and wash his feet in cocktails if he likes. That's his affair."

Thus rebuked, I say no more. And I too "save", first out of habit and then to imitate my companions, so as to excite neither their jealousy nor their contempt. Can she be Max's love, that woman with the calm, indifferent, unsociable look of those who belong neither here nor elsewhere, reflected in the smoke-blackened mirror of a "Brasserie Lorraine" where she is dining, that traveller with the dark-ringed eyes, a travelling veil knotted under her chin, and everything about her, from her hat to her boots, the colour of the road? Can she be Max's lover, the pale lover whom he used to embrace half-naked in a rose-coloured kimono, that tired comedienne who comes along, in corset and petticoat, to hunt in Brague's trunk for her chemise, her linen for the next day, and to put away her spangled draperies?

Every day I wait for my love's letter. Every day it consoles me and disappoints me at the same time. He writes simply but obviously not with ease. His beautiful flowery writing slows up the natural impetus of his hand. And then his tenderness and his sadness both constrain him, as he ingenuously laments: "When I've told you a hundred times that I love you and that I'm horribly cross with you for having left me, what more can I say? My darling wife, my little blue-stocking of a wife, you'll laugh at me but I don't care. My brother is leaving for the Ardennes and I'm going with him. Write to me at Salles-Neuves, care of my mother. I'm going to collect some money, some money for us, for our home, little sweetheart."

This is the way he tells me of his doings and what is happening to him, with no commentary and without frills. He associates me with his life and calls me his wife. He has no idea that by the time his warm solicitude reaches me it has become no more than a beautifully even writing, all cold on the paper; so far apart, what help to us are words? One needs—oh, I don't know—perhaps some passionate drawing, all glowing with colour.

f o u r

April 11th.

"**S**O NOW YOU'RE GETTING BLANDINE TO TELL YOUR FORTUNE *from the cards! This really is the limit. My darling, you're lost. Whenever I leave the house, that girl always prophesies the most picturesque catastrophes. If I go on tour she dreams of cats and serpents, turbid waters and folded sheets, and reads in the cards the tragic· adventures of Renée Néré (the Queen of Clubs) with the False Young Man, the Soldier and the Rustic. Don't listen to her, Max. Count the days as I do, and smile—oh, that smile that makes hardly perceptible wrinkles in your nostrils—to think that the first week is almost over.*

"*I myself prophesy to you that, in one month and four days, I shall 'steer my course' to rejoin the 'Big-hearted Man' and that 'you will have great joy of it' and that the False Young Man will be 'thwarted', as will also the mysterious 'Woman of Ill-Fame', by whom I mean the Queen of Diamonds.*

"*Here we are for five days at Lyons. That'll be a rest, did you say? Yes, if by that you mean that for four mornings running I shall be able to wake up with a start at daybreak, scared to death of missing my train, and then fall back on my bed in a state of exhausted laziness that drives sleep away, and listen for a long time to the servants getting up round me, to the bells, and the traffic in the street. It is much worse, my darling, than the daily departure at dawn. I have the impression that I'm looking on, from the depths of my bed, at a fresh start from which I'm excluded, that the world is*

174
......

beginning to 'turn' without me. And then it is in the depths of my bed, too, when I'm a prey to my memories and overcome with boredom, that I most long for you.

"O dear enemy, we might have spent five days together here. Don't mistake this for a challenge; I don't want you to come. Don't worry, I shan't die of it, lord no! You always seem to think that being away from you has killed me already. My handsome peasant, all it does is to benumb me, I'm hibernating.

"It's stopped raining and it's mild and damp grey, the best kind of Lyons weather. It's rather absurd, the way these meteorological reports crop up in all my letters, but if you only knew how, on tour, both our fate and our moods hang on the colour of the sky. 'Wet weather, dry pocket,' says Brague.

"In the last four years I've spent seven or eight weeks in Lyons. My first visit was to see the deer in the park of Saint-Jean, those little blonde fawns with their unseeing, tender gaze. There are so many of them, and all so alike, that I can't single one out; they follow me down the length of the wire-netting with a trot which pits the soil like hail, and beg black bread with clear, persistent, timid bleats. The smell of the turf, of the churned-up earth, is so strong in this garden, under the still air at the end of the day, that it would be able to carry me back to you if I attempted to escape.

"Goodbye, darling. Here in Lyons I've run again into some wanderers of my own sort whom I met here or elsewhere. If I were to tell you that one is called Cavaillon, a comic singer, and the other Amalia Barally, who plays the duennas in comedies, you wouldn't be much the wiser. Yet Barally is almost a friend, for we played together in a three-act play all round France, two years ago. She is a one-time beauty, a dark woman with a Roman face, an accomplished trouper, who knows by name every inn in the world. She has sung in operetta in Saigon, acted in comedies in Cairo, and enlivened the evenings of I don't know what khedive.

"What I appreciate in her, in addition to her gaiety which is proof against poverty, is her protective nature, that skill in looking after people, a delicate motherliness in her gestures which you find in women who have sincerely and passionately loved women; it confers on them an indefinable attraction which you men will never perceive.

"Heavens, how I write to you! I could spend my whole time writing to you, I believe I find it easier to write than to talk to you. Take me in your arms; it's nearly dark now, the worst moment of the day; hold me very close, very close.

Your
Renée."

April 15th.

"My darling, how kind of you! What a good idea. Thank you, thank you with all my heart for that badly-developed snapshot, yellow with hyposulphite; you're both there, my dear ones, ravishing, the pair of you. And now of course I can't any longer scold you for having taken Fossette to Salles-Neuves without my permission. She looks so happy in your arms. She's put on her photograph face, that makes her look like a beefy wrestler, holder of the Gold Belt.

"It's clear—as I observe with a slightly jealous gratitude—that at that moment she had no thoughts at all for me. But what about your eyes, that I can't see because they're gazing paternally down at Fossette, what were they dreaming about? The tender awkwardness of your arms holding that little dog both moves and amuses me. I slip this portrait of you, with the two others, into the old leather pocketbook—you remember?—which you thought had a mysterious and sinister air.

"Send me still more photos, will you? I've brought four with me and I compare them, examining you in them with a magnifying glass, to find again in each one, notwithstanding the smears of the retouching and the exaggerated lighting, a little of your secret self. Secret? Heavens no, there's nothing deceptive in you. It seems to me that any little goose would know you at a glance, as I do.

"I say that, you know, but I don't believe a word of it. Behind my teasing there's a nasty little desire to simplify you, to humiliate in *you the old adversary: that's what I've always called the man who is destined to possess me.*

"*Is it true there are so many anemones in your woods, and violets? I saw some violets near Nancy when I was crossing that undulating eastern countryside, blue with firs and slashed with bright, sparkling rivers where the water is green-black. Was that you, that tall boy bare-legged in the icy water, fishing for trout?*

"*Goodbye. Tomorrow we leave for Saint-Etienne. I must grumble to you about Hamond, who hardly ever writes to me, so you must try and write to me a lot, my dear, in case I should complain to Hamond. I kiss you.*

Renée."

five

WE HAVE JUST DINED AT BERTHOUX'S—AN ARTISTES' RES-taurant—Barally, Cavaillon, Brague, I and the Troglodyte, whom I had invited. He does not talk, his one idea is to eat. It was a typical "barnstormers' " dinner, noisy but with rather a false gaiety. Cavaillon stood us a bottle of Moulin-à-Vent.

"You must be horribly bored here," chaffed Brague, "to fork up the price of such a classy wine."

"I'll say," replied Cavaillon briefly.

Cavaillon, young but already famous in the music-hall world, is envied by everyone there. They say of him that "Dranem is afraid of him", and that "he earns whatever he chooses". We have run into this tall young man of twenty-two once or twice already; he walks like a human serpent, as though he had no bones, his heavy fists swinging at the end of his frail wrists. His face, under his fair hair cut in a fringe, is almost pretty, but his mauve glance, anxious and restless, re-veals acute neurasthenia, near to madness. His favourite ex-pression is: "I'm killing myself." He spends his whole day waiting till it is time for his act, and while it lasts he forgets, enjoys himself, and carries the public away. He neither drinks nor goes on the loose. He invests his money and is bored.

Barally, who is "spinning out" a season at the *Celestins*, has laughed so much, showing her beautiful teeth, and talked so much, relating terrific binges when she was young, that it has gone to her head. She tells us of the colonial theatres of twenty years ago, when she used to sing in operetta in Saigon, in a hall lit by eight hundred oil lamps. Penniless and already old, she is the old-fashioned Bohemian incarnate, likeable and incorrigible.

A pleasant dinner all the same: we work each other up and come close together for an instant round the over-small table, and then goodbye. A goodbye without regrets, for the next day, or the next moment, we forget each other. . . . At last we are off again. Five days in Lyons can be interminable.

Cavaillon accompanies us to the Kursaal; it is too early for him since he only takes ten minutes to make up; but, a prey to solitude and grown silent and gloomy again, he clings to us. The Troglodyte, transported and slightly tipsy, sings to the stars, and I dream, and listen to the black wind rising and sweeping up the banks of the Rhone with a roar like the sea. Why do I feel as though I were rocked on an invisible swell like a ship set afloat by the sea? It is the kind of evening that makes one want to sail to the other side of the world. My cheeks are cold, my ears frozen and my nose moist: my whole animal self feels fit and vigorous and adventurous . . . until we get to the threshold of the Kursaal, where the musty warmth of the basement chokes my cleansed lungs.

As glum as government clerks, we arrive at those peculiar artists' dressing-rooms which resemble at the same time lofts in provincial houses, and servants' attics, papered in cheap grey and white. Cavaillon, who shed us on the staircase, is already in his dressing-room where I see him, sitting before his make-up shelf, his elbows propped on it and his head in his hands. Brague tells me that that is how this comic actor passes his lugubrious evenings, utterly worn out and silent. I shiver. I should like to shake off the memory of that man sitting there and hiding his face. I am afraid of becoming like him, that wretched, stranded creature, lost in our midst and conscious of his solitude.

179

s i x

April 18th.

"**Y**OU'RE AFRAID I'M FORGETTING YOU? *That's a new idea!
Max darling, don't start 'playing the tart', as I call it. I
think of you and gaze at you from far off with such keen
attention that you ought, every now and again, to feel some mysterious intimation of it. Don't you? Across the distance that separates us
I watch you intently, unwearyingly. I see you so clearly. The hours of
our rapid intimacy have now yielded up all their secrets to me, and I
slowly unfold all our words, all our silences, our looks and our gestures, faithfully recorded with all their pictorial and musical values.
And this is the time you choose to complain coquettishly, a finger in
the corner of your mouth: 'You're forgetting me, I feel you've gone
further away from me!' Really, the second sight of lovers!*

"*It is true I'm going further away, my dear. We have just left
Avignon behind, and when I woke in the train yesterday after a nap
of two hours, I might have thought I had slept for two months;
spring had come to meet me, a spring such as one imagines in fairy-
tales, the exuberant, ephemeral, irresistible spring of the South, rich
and fresh, springing up in sudden bursts of greenery, in plants already tall which sway and ripple in the wind, in mauve Judas trees
and paulownias the colour of grey periwinkles, in laburnums, wis-
tarias and roses.*

"*The first roses, my dear one! I bought them in the station at
Avignon, little more than buds, of sulphur yellow touched with carmine, transparent in the sun as an ear aglow with bright blood,*

adorned with tender leaves and curved thorns of polished coral. They are on my table now. They smell like apricot and vanilla, like a very fine cigar, and like some dark, curled and scented beauty—the exact scent, Max, of your dry, dark-skinned hands.

"Dear one, I'm letting myself be dazzled and revived by this new season, this hard, strong sky, and that rare, gold colour of rocks that have been caressed by the sun all the year round. No, no, don't pity me for leaving at dawn, since dawn in this country breaks, naked and rosy, from a milky sky, filled with the sound of bells and flights of white pigeons. . . . Oh I beseech you, do understand that you mustn't write me 'thought out' letters, that you mustn't think of what you are writing to me. Write no matter what, the kind of weather you're having, what time you woke up, how cross you feel with your 'salaried gipsy'; fill your pages with the same tender word, repeated like the cry of a mating bird. My dear lover, I want you to feel the same disturbance as this spring which has thrust its way out of the earth and is burning itself up with its own haste."

I rarely re-read my letters, but I've re-read this one and let it go with the strange impression that I was doing a clumsy thing, making a mistake, and that it was on its way to a man who ought not to have read it. I have felt a bit light-headed since we left Avignon. The regions of mist have melted away behind the curtains of cypress that bend under the mistral. That day the silky rustle of the long reeds came in through the lowered window of the compartment, together with a scent of honey and pine, of varnished buds and unopened lilac, that bitter scent of the lilac before it flowers, like turpentine and almond mingled. The cherry trees cast a violet shadow on the reddish earth already cracking with thirst. The train cuts across or runs along beside white roads where a chalky dust rolls in low clouds and powders the bushes. A pleasantly exciting murmur, like that of a distant swarm of bees, buzzes incessantly in my ears.

Alive to that excess of scent and colour and warmth, and

unable to resist although I had foreseen it, I let myself be taken by surprise, carried away and conquered. Can it be that there is no danger in such sweetness?

Below the balcony, the deafening Canebière teems at my feet, that Canebière which rests neither day nor night, and where idling takes on the importance and assurance of a job. If I bend forward I can see the water of the port glittering at the end of the street behind the geometrical lace of the riggings, a fragment of dark blue sea dancing in little short waves.

My hand, on the edge of the balcony, crumbles the last note from my love, in answer to my letter from Lyons. Unluckily he recalls from it that my comrade Amalia Barally was not a lover of men and, like the "normal" and "well-balanced" being that he is, he has not failed to cast a bit of a slur on my old friend, by poking fun at her, and to vilify something that he does not understand. What would be the good of explaining to him? Two women enlaced will never be for him anything but a depraved couple, he will never see in them the melancholy and touching image of two weak creatures who have perhaps sought shelter in each other's arms, there to sleep and weep, safe from man who is so often cruel, and there to taste, better than any pleasure, the bitter happiness of feeling themselves akin, frail and forgotten. What would be the good of writing, and pleading, and discussing? My voluptuous friend can only understand love.

seven

April 24th.

"DON'T DO THAT, I IMPLORE YOU, DON'T DO THAT! Landing here without a word of warning, you haven't seriously thought of it, have you?

"What should I do if I saw you suddenly entering my dressing-room, as you did five months ago at the Empyrée-Clichy? Goodness me, I should keep you here, you can be sure of that. But that is why you mustn't come. I should keep you, my darling, against my heart, against my breast that you have so often caressed, against my mouth which is wilting from not being kissed any more. Ah, how I should keep you! That is why you must not come.

"Stop invoking our common need of taking fresh courage, of drawing from each other the strength for a new separation. Let me devote myself wholly to my job, which you do not like. After all, it's only twenty days more before I return. Let me finish my tour, putting into it an almost soldierly sense of duty and that sort of honest worker's application with which one mustn't mix our happiness. Your letter frightened me, my darling. I thought I was going to see you walk in. Take care not to overwhelm your love and do not lavish on her unexpected sorrows, or joys either.

Renée."

183

The canvas awning flaps above our heads, chequering with light and shade the terrace of the restaurant on the port where we have just been lunching. Brague reads the newspapers, uttering exclamations from time to time and talking to himself. I don't hear him, I scarcely see him. A habit already of long standing has suppressed all politeness, coquetry and modesty between us—all the insincere things. We have just been eating sea-urchins, tomatoes, and a *brandade* of cod. In front of us, between the oily sea lapping the sides of the boats and the perforated wooden balustrade which encloses this terrace, there is a stretch of pavement where busy people with the happy faces of idlers pass up and down; there are fresh flowers, carnations tied up in stiff bunches, like leeks, soaking in green pails; there is a street-stall loaded with black bananas smelling of ether, and shell-fish dripping with sea-water: sea-urchins, *"violets"*, clams, blue mussels and cockles, dotted about with lemons and little flasks of pink vinegar.

I cool my hand on the belly of the white water-cooler, ribbed like a melon, which stands exuding moisture on the table. Everything there belongs to me and possesses me. I shall not think tomorrow that I am taking this picture away with me, but it seems to me that a shadow of myself, detached from me like a leaf, will remain here, a little bowed with fatigue, its transparent hand stretched out and laid on the side of an invisible water-cooler.

I contemplate my changing kingdom as though I had almost lost it. Yet nothing threatens this easy, wandering life, nothing, except a letter. It is there, in my little bag. My word, how my love writes when he wants to! How clearly he makes himself understood! Here, in eight pages, is something that I can at last call a real love-letter. It has the incoherence of a love-letter, the spelling groggy in places, the tenderness and . . . the authority. A superb authority which disposes of me, my future, and the whole of my little life. Absence has done its work; he has suffered without me and so he has thought things out and carefully planned a lasting happiness: he offers me marriage as if he were offering me a sunny enclosure, bounded by solid walls.

"My mother certainly cried a little, but I let her cry. She has always done what I wanted. You will win her heart, and besides, we shan't be spending much time with her. You love travelling, don't you, my darling wife? You shall have so much that you'll get tired of it; the whole world shall be yours, until you come to love nothing but a little corner of our own where you will no longer be Renée Néré but My Lady Wife. You'll have to be content to be billed as that in future! I'm already arranging to . . ."

What is he already arranging? I unfold the thin sheets of foreign writing-paper which rustle like bank notes: he is arranging to move, since the second floor of his brother's house was never suitable for anything but a bachelor flat. He has his eye on something in the neighbourhood of the *Rue Pergolèse*.

Impelled by a cruel hilarity, I crumple the letter, exclaiming to myself: "That's all very well, but what about me, am I not to be consulted? What do I become in all that?"

Brague raises his head, then takes up his paper again, without a word. It takes more than that to startle him out of his discretion, which is part reserve and part indifference.

I was not lying when I wrote to Max two days ago: "I see you so clearly, now that I'm far away." I only hope I do not see him too clearly. Young, too young for me, idle, free, affectionate, but spoilt: "My mother has always done what I wanted." I hear his voice pronouncing those words, his beautiful sombre voice with its seductive modulations, as though he had learnt in the theatre how to use it, that voice which gives beauty to the words, and I hear, like a diabolical echo, another voice which rises, muffled, from the depths of my memories: "The woman who will order me about is not yet born." Coincidence, if you will, but all the same it seems to me as though I had just swallowed a small piece of sharp glass.

Yes, what do I become in all that? A happy woman? This sunlight, imperiously penetrating the "dark room" of my inmost being, makes it difficult to think.

"I'm going in, Brague, I'm tired."

Brague looks at me over the top of his paper, his head on one side to avoid the thread of smoke rising from the half-extinguished cigarette in the corner of his mouth.

"Tired? Not ill? It's Saturday you know. The public at the *Eldo* will be pretty lively, so keep up to the mark."

I don't deign to answer. Does he take me for a beginner? We know all about this Marseilles public, decent but excitable, despising timidity and punishing conceit, not to be won over unless one throws one's whole self into it.

The migraine which was beginning vanishes as I get un-dressed and feel on my skin the coolness of a bluish shantung kimono, that has been washed twenty times. I do not lie down on my bed, for fear of going to sleep; I have not come here to rest. Kneeling on an armchair against the open window, I prop my elbows on the back of it and rub my bare feet against each other behind me. A few days ago I fell again into the habit of planking myself down on the edge of a table, perching on the arm of an easy chair, and remaining for a long time in awk-ward attitudes on uncomfortable seats, as though for these brief pauses on my way it was not worth while installing my-self, or taking trouble to rest properly. Anyone might think that, with my coat thrown here and my hat there, I was only spending a quarter of an hour in the bedrooms where I sleep. It is in railway carriages that I show myself to be methodical to the point of mania, surrounded by my handbag, my rolled rug, my books and papers, the rubber cushions which support me when, with the promptitude of a hardened traveller, I fall into a rigid sleep which disturbs neither my veil, tied like a nun's head-band, nor my skirt drawn down to my ankles.

I am not resting. I want to force myself to think, and my mind jibs, escapes, darts down a path of light that a sunbeam, falling on the balcony, opens before it, and goes on its way across a mosaic roof of green tiles down below, where it childishly stops to play with a reflection, the shadow of a cloud. I struggle, lashing myself on. Then I give up for a minute, only to begin again. It is duels such as this which give to exiles like me those wide-open eyes, so slow to detach their gaze from some invisible lure. These are the gloomy gymnastics of the solitary.

Solitary! How can I think such a thing when my lover is calling to me, ready to take care of me all my life long? But I don't know what "all my life long" means. Three months ago I pronounced those terrible words "ten years", "twenty years", without understanding. Now the time has come when I must understand. My lover offers me his life, the improvident and generous life of a young man of about thirty-four, like me. He thinks I am young too, and he does not see the *end* —my end. In his blindness he will not admit that I must change and grow old, although every second, added to the second that is fleeting, is already snatching me away from him.

I still have what it takes to please him, and more still, to dazzle him. I can put off this face of mine as one takes off a mask; I have another, more beautiful face, which he has glimpsed. And where others adorn themselves, I disrobe, trained as I have been, first as Taillandy's model and then as a dancer, to avoid the dangers that lie in nudity and to move naked under the light as though it was a complicated drapery. But for how many years more am I still thus armed?

My friend offers me his name and his fortune, with his love. Decidedly my master Chance is doing things handsomely, and is anxious to reward by one large gesture my desultory worship of him. It is both unexpected and crazy; it is also a bit too much!

187
......

Dear good man, he will be awaiting my reply impatiently and watching for the postman on the road, in company with Fossette, my Fossette who is thrilled at acting the Lady of the Manor, riding in a motor and playing inner circle round the saddled horses. I am sure his joy must be intensified by the naïve legitimate pride of a gentleman who has been decent enough to raise from below stage at the *Emp'-Clich'* to his own level on the white terrace of Salles-Neuves, a nice little "*caf'-conc'* " actress.

Dear, dear, heroic *bourgeois!* Ah, why doesn't he love one of his own kind? How happy she would make him! It seems to me that I shall never be able to.

If it were only a question of giving myself! But voluptuous pleasure is not the only thing. In the limitless desert of love it holds a very small place, so flaming that at first one sees nothing else; but I am not a green young girl, to be blinded by the brilliance of it. All about this flickering hearth there lies the unknown, there lies danger. What do I know of the man whom I love and who wants me? After we have risen from a short embrace, or even from a long night, we shall have to begin to live at close quarters to each other, and in dependence on each other. He will bravely hide the first disappointments that I shall cause him, and I shall keep silent about mine, out of pride and shame and pity, and above all because I shall have expected them, *because I shall recognise them.* I who shrink right up when I hear myself called "my darling child", I who tremble before certain gestures of his, certain intonations that rise up from the past, what an army of ghosts is lying in wait for me behind the curtains of a bed that is still unopened?

No reflection dances now on the green-tiled roof down below. The sun has started to sink; a lake of sky, azure a moment ago between two spindles of motionless cloud, now pales serenely, passing from turquoise to lemon-green. My arms, propped on their elbows, and my bent knees, have gone to sleep. The unprofitable day is drawing to its end and I have decided nothing and written nothing, nor have I torn from my heart one of those irresistible impulses whose wild guidance I once upon a time accepted, without further thought, ready to call it "divine".

What shall I do? For today I'll write—briefly, for time is short—and lie to him.

"My darling, it is nearly six o'clock and I've spent the whole day struggling against a terrible migraine. The heat is so great and so sudden that it makes me groan but, like Fossette before too bright a fire, without resentment. And then your letter on top of all that! You and the sky overwhelm me with your gifts, it's just too much sun, too much light at the same time; that's all I have strength for today, to sigh 'It's too much!' A friend like you, Max, and lots of love and lots of happiness and lots of money . . . how strong you must think me! I am, usually, it is true, but not today. Give me time.

"Here is a photograph for you. I've just received it from Lyons where Barally took this snapshot. Don't you think I look terribly dark and small, and sort of lost dog, with those folded hands and that beaten look? Frankly, my dear love, that humble stray feels ill-equipped to bear the excess of honour and wealth that you promise her. She is looking in your direction and her defiant fox's muzzle seems to say to you 'Is it really for me, all that? Are you sure?'

"Goodbye, my darling love. You are the best of men, and you deserved the best of wives. Will you not regret having chosen only
Renée Néré?"

I have forty-eight hours before me.

And now I must hurry and get ready to dine on the terrace at Basso's, in the cool breeze and the scent of lemons and wet mussels, and then rush to the *Eldorado* along avenues bathed in pink electric light, snapping, at last, for a few hours, the thread which unceasingly draws me away back there.

eight

Nice, Cannes, Mentone. . . . On I spin, followed by my ever-growing torment: a torment so lively, so ever-present, that I sometimes fear I may see the shape of its shadow beside mine on the pale freestone of the jetties that enclose the sea, or on the hot pavement where banana skins lie fermenting. My torment tyrannises over me; it comes between me and the joy of living, contemplating, and breathing deeply. One night I dreamt that I did not love, and that night, released from all bonds, I lay as though in a kind of soothing death.

To my ambiguous letter from Marseilles Max replied with a calm and happy one, full of thanks from beginning to end without a word crossed out, and friendly, confident love proud of giving everything and receiving more; in short a letter which might have made me suppose I had written: "On such a day, at such an hour, I will be yours and we will go away together."

Is it really settled then? Am I as much committed as that? And this bad mood which makes me find the time drag so between one day and another, one town and another, one night and another, is it due to impatience or to haste? At Mentone yesterday I was listening, in a boarding-house drowsing among gardens, to the birds and the flies waking up, and the parakeet on the balcony. The dawn wind made the palm trees rustle like dead reeds and I recognised all the sounds, the whole music, of a similar morning the year before.

But this year the whistling of the parakeet, the buzzing of the wasps as the sun rose, and the stiff breeze in the palms all receded far away from me and seemed like a murmured accompaniment to my anxiety, acting as a pedal to my obsession, love.

In the garden, under my window, an oblong bed of violets which the sun had not yet touched made a blue patch in the dew, beneath mimosas yellow as a chick. And against the wall there were climbing roses, too, which I guessed were scentless from their colour, greenish and sulphury yellow, the same indeterminate shade as the sky, which was not yet blue. The same roses and the same violets as the year before; but why was I not able to greet them yesterday with that involuntary smile, reflecting a harmless, half-physical felicity, in which the silent happiness of solitary people expresses itself?

I suffer. I cannot attach myself to what I see. For just a minute longer, just one more, I cling to what would be the greatest folly, the irremediable unhappiness of the rest of my existence. Clinging and leaning, like a tree which has grown over an abyss, and the weight of whose blossoming bends it towards its destruction, I still resist, and who can say if I shall succeed?

As soon as I grow calmer and accept the thought of my brief future, in which I shall belong utterly to the man who awaits me back there, a little picture, a little photographic picture casts me back into my torment, and into prudence. It is a snapshot of Max playing tennis with a young girl. It has no significance: the young girl is a casual acquaintance, a neighbour come for tea at Salles-Neuves, and he was not thinking of her when he sent me his photograph. But I think of her and I was already thinking of her before I saw her. I do not know her name, I can hardly see her face, turned up to the sun, and dark, with a cheerful grin revealing a shining line of white teeth. Ah, if I had my lover there at my feet, between my hands, I should say to him. . . .

No, I should say nothing to him. But to write is so easy. To

191

write, to write, to cover white pages with the rapid, uneven writing which he says is like my mobile face, exhausted from expressing too much. To write sincerely, almost sincerely! I hope it may bring me relief, that sort of interior silence which follows a sudden utterance, a confession.

"*Max, my dear love, I asked you yesterday the name of that young girl playing tennis with you. I need not have bothered. As far as I am concerned she is called* a girl, *all the girls, all the young women who will be my rivals a little later on, soon, tomorrow. She is called the unknown, my junior, the one with whom I shall be cruelly and lucidly compared, yet with less cruelty and clear-sightedness than I shall use myself.*

"*Triumph over her? How often? And what is triumph when the struggle is exhausting and never-ending? Understand me, please understand me! It is not suspicion, not your future betrayal, my love, which is devastating me, it is my own inadequacy. We are the same age; I am no longer a young woman. Oh my love, imagine yourself in a few years' time, as a handsome man in the fullness of your age, beside me in mine! Imagine me, still beautiful but desperate, frantic in my armour of corset and frock, under my make-up and powder, in my young, tender colours. Imagine me, beautiful as a full-blown rose which one must not touch. A glance of yours, resting on a young woman, will be enough to lengthen the sad crease that smiling has engraved on my cheek, but a happy night in your arms will cost my fading beauty dearer still. I am reaching—you know it—the age of ardour. It is the age of fatal imprudences. Understand me! Will not your fervour, if I let it convince and reassure me, lead me into the fatuous security of women who are loved? I have seen satisfied, amo-rous women in whom, for a few brief and dangerous minutes, the affected ingénue reappears and allows herself girlish tricks which make her rich and heavy flesh quiver. I have shuddered at the lack of awareness of a friend in her forties who, unclothed and all breath-less with love, clapped on her head the cap of her lover, a lieutenant of Hussars.*

"*Yes, I know, I'm rambling, and frightening you. You don't understand. What this letter lacks is a long preamble containing all the thoughts I am hiding from you, the thoughts that have been poisoning me for so long. Love is so simple, isn't it? You never supposed it had this ambiguous, tormented face? We love and give ourselves to each other, and there we are, happy for life, isn't that it? Ah, how young you are, and worse than young, you whose only suffering is waiting for me! Your hell is limited to not possessing what you desire, a thing which some people have to put up with all their lives. But to possess what one loves and every minute to feel one's sole treasure disintegrating, melting, and slipping away like gold dust between one's fingers! And not to have the dreadful courage to open one's hand and let the whole treasure go, but to clench one's fingers ever tighter, and to cry and beg to keep . . . what? a precious little trace of gold in the hollow of one's palm.*

"*Don't you understand? My little one, I would give anything in the world to resemble you, I wish I might never have suffered except because of you, and that I could fling away my old, well-tried distress. Help your Renée, as you can if you will, but, my love, if I no longer hope except in you, am I not already half-way to despair?*"

My hand still grips the wretched, over-thin pen-holder. On the table, four large sheets of paper bear witness to the haste with which I have written, no less than does the untidiness of the manuscript where the writing slopes upwards and downwards, sometimes bigger and sometimes smaller, responsive to my mood. Will he be able to make me out in all this untidiness? No. I am still concealed in it. To speak the truth is one thing, but the whole truth, that cannot, must not, be said.

Before me, on the square, swept by a wind which was keen a short while back but now weakens and drops like a tired wing, the arched wall of the arena at Nîmes rears its red-brown, rugose substance against a stretch of opaque, slate-coloured sky which foretells a storm. The burning air drifts about my room. I want to see again, under this heavy sky, my Elysian refuge, the Gardens of the Fountain.

A ramshackle cab and a worn-out horse take me as far as the

black railings which protect this park where nothing changes. Can last year's spring have lasted magically until this hour, to wait for me? It is so fairy-like in this place, where the spring hangs motionless over all things, that I tremble lest I should see it swallowed up and melt into a cloud.

Amorously, my hand caresses the warm stone of the ruined temple and the varnished leaves of the spindle-trees, which seem damp. The baths of Diana, over which I lean, still, as always, reflect the Judas trees, the terebinths, the pines, the paulownias with their mauve flowers, and the double purple thorns. A whole garden of reflections is spread out there below me, turning, as it decomposes in the aquamarine water, dark blue, the violet of a bruised peach, and the maroon of dried blood. Oh beautiful garden and beautiful silence, where the only sound is the muted plashing of the green, imperious water, transparent and dark, blue and brilliant as a bright dragon.

A harmonious double alley, between walls of clipped yew, leads up to the Tour Magne, and I stop to rest for a moment on the edge of a stone trough full of stagnant water, green with fine watercress and chattering tree-frogs with tiny delicate hands. At the top, the very top, a dry bed of scented pine-needles receives us, me and my torment.

The beautiful garden lies spread out below, with open spaces in a geometrical design. The approach of the storm has driven away all intruders, and the hurricane, with its hail, rises slowly from the horizon, borne along in the billowing flanks of a thick cloud rimmed with white fire.

All this is still my kingdom, a small portion of the splendid riches which God distributes to passers-by, to wanderers and to solitaries. The earth belongs to anyone who stops for a moment, gazes and goes on his way; the whole sun belongs to the naked lizard who basks in it.

Underlying all my anxiety there is a great bargaining going on, a kind of bartering which weighs up undisclosed values and half-hidden treasures; and this dispute is slowly rising up and forcing its way into the daylight. Time presses. The whole truth, which I could not tell to Max, I owe to myself. It is not a beautiful truth, and it is still a bit feeble and scared, and slightly perfidious. So far all it can do is to whisper to me in short sighs: "I don't want . . . I mustn't . . . I'm afraid."

Afraid of getting old, of being betrayed, of suffering. A subtle choice guided my partial sincerity while I was writing that to Max. That particular fear is the hair-shirt which clings to the skin of nascent Love and contracts there as he grows. I have worn that hair-shirt; one does not die of it. I would wear it again if . . . *if I could not do otherwise.*

"If I could not do otherwise. . . ." This time the formula is clear. I saw it written in my mind and I see it there still, printed like a judgment in small, bold capitals. Now at last I have taken the true measure of my paltry love and brought my real hope into the open: the hope of escape.

But how to achieve it? Everything is against me. The first obstacle I run into is the female body lying there, which bars my way, a voluptuous body with closed eyes, deliberately blind, stretched out and ready to perish rather than leave the place where its joy lies. That woman there, that brute bent on pleasure, is I myself. "You are your own worst enemy." Don't I know it, my word, don't I know it! Shall I also be able to overcome the lost child, a hundred times more dangerous than that greedy beast, who trembles inside me, weak and nervous and ready to stretch out her arms and implore: "Don't leave me alone!" She is afraid, that child, of night, solitude, illness and death, in the evenings she draws the curtains over the dark window pane which frightens her, and pines merely because she is not cherished enough. And you, Max, my well-beloved adversary, how will lacerating myself help me to get the better of you? You would only have to appear and . . . But I am not calling to you to come!

No, I am not calling to you to come. It is my first victory.

* * *

Now the stormy cloud is passing over my head, letting fall, one by one, sluggish, scented drops of water. A star of rain plops on the corner of my mouth and I drink it, warm and sweetened with a dust that tastes of jonquils.

nine

Nîmes, Montpellier, Carcassonne, Toulouse . . . four days without respite, and four nights. We arrive, wash, eat, dance to the accompaniment of an orchestra reading at sight and not sure of itself, go to bed—is it worth while?—and leave again. We grow thin with weariness and no one complains, pride before everything. We change music-halls, dressing-rooms, hotels and rooms with the indifference of soldiers on manoeuvres. The make-up box is peeling and showing its tin. The costumes are beginning to wear and, hastily cleaned with petrol before the show, give out a sour smell of rice-powder and cleaning-spirit. I re-paint with carmine my cracked sandals for *The Pursuit;* my tunic for *The Dryad* is losing its acid, grass-green, grasshopper shade. Brague is superb in dirt of all colours: his Bulgarian breeches of embroidered leather, stiff with the artificial blood which spatters them each night, look like the hide of a newly-skinned ox. The Old Troglodyte spreads terror on the stage in a tow-wig which is moulting and some discoloured and evil-smelling hare-skins.

Hard days indeed, where we gasp between a blue sky swept with occasional long clouds, wispy as though they had been frayed by the mistral, and an earth cracking and splitting with thirst. And besides, I have a double burden to bear. My two companions, when they land in a new town, free their shoulders from the strap that bows them, and then, light of heart, think of nothing but a foaming half-pint and an aimless stroll.

But for me there is the hour when the post arrives. The post: that means Max's letters.

In the glass-fronted rack and on the greasy tables where the porter scatters the papers with the back of his hand, I see, immediately and electrically, the round, flowery script and the bluish envelope: farewell to rest!

"Give it me, that one! Yes, yes, I tell you it's for me." Oh my goodness, what will there be in it? Reproaches, prayers, or perhaps merely: "I'm coming . . ."

I have waited four days for Max's reply to my letter from Nîmes; and for four days I have written tenderly to him, hiding my profound agitation under a wordy gentleness, as though I had forgotten that letter from Nîmes. At such a distance any epistolary dialogue is bound to be disjointed, and a sad note creeps in by fits and starts when things happen not to go well. Four days have I waited for Max's answer, and felt impatient and ungrateful when all I found was the tall, old-fashioned, graceful Italian hand of my friend Margot, the microscopic scribble of my old Hamond, and Blandine's postcards.

Ah, that letter from Max, I've got it at last, and I read it with a too-familiar palpitation, made more painful by a certain memory: was there not a period in my life when Taillandy "the man whom no woman ever dropped", as he always said, got suddenly furious at my absence and my silence and wrote me lover's letters? The mere sight of his spiky writing used to make me turn pale, and I would feel my heart bounding about like something very small and hard and round—just like today, just like today.

What if I were to crumble up this letter from Max without reading it, fill my lungs with air like a hanged man taken down in time, and flee? But I can't. It was only a passing temptation. I must read.

Thank my stars, my friend has not understood. He thought the whole trouble was a fit of jealousy, the coquettish alarm of a woman who wants to receive, from the man she loves, an explicit assurance in the most flattering terms. And so he gives me this assurance and I cannot help smiling because he praises his "beloved soul", sometimes as though she were a very respected sister, and sometimes as though she were a beautiful mare. "You will always be the most beautiful!" he writes, and no doubt he thinks it too. But could he answer anything else? Perhaps, at the moment of writing those words, he raised his head and looked at the deep forest before him, with a hardly perceptible hesitation, a suspension of thought. And then he will have shaken his shoulders, as one does when one is cold, and written bravely and slowly: "You will always be the most beautiful!"

Poor Max! The best of myself seems to conspire against him now. The day before yesterday we left before dawn and, as soon as we were in the train, I was just resuming my shattered sleep, broken and begun again twenty times, when a breath of salt air smelling of fresh seaweed made me open my eyes again: the sea! Sète and the sea! There it was again, running along beside the train, when I had quite forgotten it. The seven o'clock sun, still low on the horizon, had not yet penetrated it; the sea was refusing to let itself be possessed and, hardly awake, still kept its nocturnal colour of ink-blue crested with white.

Salt-pans filed past, edged with grass glittering with salt, and sleeping villas, white as the salt, between their dark laurels, their lilacs and their Judas trees. Half asleep, like the sea, and yielding to the swaying of the train, I thought I was skimming the waves, so close at hand, with a swallow's cutting flight. And then I experienced one of those perfect moments, the kind of happiness that comes to a sick person, unable to think, when a sudden *memory*, an image, a name, turned me once again into an ordinary creature, the creature of yesterday and the days before. How long had it lasted, that moment when for the first time I had forgotten Max? Yes, forgotten him, as though I had never known his gaze, nor the caress of his mouth, forgotten him as if the one dominating anxiety in my life were to seek for words, words to express how yellow the sun is, how blue the sea, and how brilliant the salt like a fringe of white jet. Yes, forgotten him, as if the only urgent thing in the world were my desire to possess through my eyes the marvels of the earth.

In that same hour an insidious spirit whispered to me: "And if indeed that were the only urgent thing? If everything, save that, were merely ashes?"

t e n

I LIVE IN A TURMOIL OF THOUGHTS WHICH GO ROUND AND round unceasingly, and only with difficulty and patience do I find again my vocation of silence and dissimulation. Once more it is easy for me to follow Brague across a town, from top to bottom, through squares, cathedrals and museums, and into the smoke of little taverns where "one eats amazingly well". Our form of cordiality speaks little and rarely smiles, but sometimes shouts with laughter as if gaiety came more naturally to us than gentleness. I laugh easily at Brague's stories and make my laughter as shrill as I can, just as he, when he speaks to me, exaggerates a coarseness that is quite unnatural.

We are both sincere but not always very simple. We have time-honoured jests which provoke time-honoured amusement: Brague's favourite—which exasperates me—is the Game of the Satyr, which is played in trams, where my comrade chooses as a victim sometimes a timid young woman and sometimes an aggressive old maid. Sitting opposite her and lolling back, he fixes a lustful gaze on her to make her blush and cough, fidget with her veil and turn her head aside. The "satyr's" look persists, lasciviously, and then all the features of his face—mouth, nostrils, eyebrows—combine to express the particular joy of an erotomaniac.

"It's a wonderful facial exercise," Brague declares. "When the Conservatoire founds a miming class for me, I shall make all my feminine pupils rehearse it together and separately."

COLETTE

I laughed because the poor scared lady never fails to leave
the tram very quickly, but the grimacing perfection of the
wicked game gets on my nerves. My body, rather exhausted,
has fits of unreasonable chastity, out of which I fall into a
brazier lit in a second by the remembrance of a scent, a gesture or a tender cry, a brazier which kindles delights which I
have not had and in whose flames I let myself be consumed,
motionless and with my knees together, as though at the
slightest movement I were in danger of enlarging my burns.

Max. . . . He writes to me and waits for me. How hard to
bear his trustfulness is! Harder to bear than to deceive, for I
too write, with a fullness and a freedom difficult to explain. I
write on wobbly pedestal tables, sitting sideways on chairs that
are too high, I write with one foot shod and one bare, the
paper lodged between the breakfast tray and my open handbag, all among the brushes, the bottle of scent and the button-
hook; I write sitting at a window that frames part of a courtyard, or the most delicious gardens, or misty mountains. I feel
myself at home amid this disorder of a camp, this no matter
where and no matter how, and freer than among my haunted
furniture.

eleven

"SOUTH AMERICA, WHAT D'YOU SAY TO THAT?"

This odd question from Brague fell like a stone yesterday into my after-dinner reverie, during that brief hour when I struggle against sleep and my reluctance to undress and put on my make-up just when I'm in the middle of digesting.

"South America? That's a long way away."

"Slacker!"

"You don't understand, Brague. I say 'it's a long way away' as I would say 'it's beautiful'."

"Oh well, all right if that's it. Salomon's been sounding me about going there. Well?"

"Well?"

"Can we consider it?"

"We can consider it."

Neither of us is taken in by our feigned indifference. I have learnt, to my cost, not to "put ideas" into the impresario's head about a tour, by showing my eagerness to go. Brague, on the other hand, unfailingly takes care not to present the matter to me in an advantageous light, for fear I will ask for a greater share of "the gross fee".

South America! At the sound of those two words I felt the dazzlement of an illiterate person who sees the New World through an enchanted web of falling stars, giant flowers, precious stones and humming birds. Brazil, the Argentine . . .

what glittering names! Margot told me that she was taken there when she was quite small, and the longing and amazement she evoked remain fixed to the picture she gave me of a spider with a silver stomach and a tree covered with fireflies.

Brazil, the Argentine, but . . . what about Max?

What about Max? Ever since yesterday I've been prowling round this question mark. What about Max? What about Max? It is no longer a thought, it is a refrain, a noise, a little rhythmic croaking which inevitably brings on one of my "fits of coarseness". Who is the foul-mouthed ancestor who goes on barking inside me with a violence not only verbal but sentimental? I have just crumpled up the letter I had begun to my love, swearing under my breath.

"What about Max! What about Max! What, again? However long am I going to go on finding this creature getting under my feet? What about Max! What about Max! What about me, then, do I merely exist to bother my head about this cumbersome capitalist? A truce, Lord, I beseech you, I've had enough fusses and idylls and lost time, and enough of men! Look at yourself, my poor girl, look at yourself, you're not an old woman, by a long chalk, but you're already a kind of confirmed bachelor. You've got the fads of such, and the difficult character, and the finicking sensibility—enough of them to cause you suffering and make you unbearable. What will you do in that galley, or rather in that tub of a houseboat, firmly moored, in solemn attendance on the master's needs? If you could just manage to indulge in a nice little infatuation for the chap, say fifteen days, three weeks or two months and then goodbye! No strings on either side, just a mutual enjoyment. You ought to have learnt, when you were with Taillandy, how to drop people!"

On and on I rant. I display a crude and wicked ingenuity in finding ways to insult my friend and myself; it is a kind of game in which I provoke myself to say true things that I do not think, that I have not so far thought. And it goes on until the moment when I notice that it is raining in torrents: the roofs on the other side of the road are streaming, and the gutter overflowing. A long, cold water-drop rolls down the window and falls on my hand. Behind me the room has grown dark. How good it would be to lean now against the shoulder of the man I was humiliating a moment ago by calling him a cumbersome capitalist.

I switch on the ceiling-light and, for something to do, try a temporary arrangement of the writing-table, opening the blotter between the cheval-glass and the bunch of narcissus; I'm trying to make the place look like home and what I long for is hot tea, golden bread, my familiar lamp with its pink shade, the barking of my dog and the voice of my old Hamond. A large sheet of white paper lying there tempts me, and I sit down:

"Max, my darling, yes, I'm coming back; I return a little every day. Is it possible that only twelve nights separate me from you? Nothing is less sure; it seems to me that I shall never see you again. How terrible that would be! And how wise!"

I stop short: is it not too clear? No. Besides, I wrote "it would be", and no lover would ever take a conditional tragically. I can continue in the same reassuring vein, risking a few melancholy generalities and a few timorous taboos. And since, all the same, I dread a brusque decision which would bring Max here in less than twelve hours, I do not forget to drown the whole letter in a flood of tenderness which, alas, draw me on.

Rather disgusting, all that.

t w e l v e

How time flies! Where are the Pyrenees with their blossoming cherries, the great austere mountain which seemed to follow us, glittering with a snow which makes you thirsty, slashed with vertiginous shadows, rent with blue chasms and blotched with bronze forests? Where are the narrow valleys, turf-carpeted, and the wild orchids white as gardenias, and where the little Basque village square where we drank steaming dark chocolate? How far away already is the icy Gave, that graceful dangerous river with its waters clouded by the melting of the snows to the milky transparency of moonstones!

We are leaving Bordeaux now, after giving five shows in three days. "A nice town," sighed Brague at the station. "I treated myself to a little Bordelaise . . . a dainty dish! One of those small helpings you can get for the asking in all the main streets, can't you just see? High as your heart, plenty of breast, short in the leg, a plump little foot, and so plastered with eye-black and powder and frizzed hair that I defy you to tell whether they're pretty or not. They sparkle and chatter and wriggle—they're just my dish!"

He exuded tranquil happiness and I looked at him with a rather disgusted hostility, as I look at people eating when I am no longer hungry.

The timid spring flees before us, growing younger hour by hour and closing again leaf by leaf and flower by flower as we get further north. In the sparser shade of the hedges, the April daisies have reappeared, and the last faded violets. The paler blue of the sky, the shorter grass and an acid humidity in the air give one the illusion of growing younger and going back in time.

If only I could wind back again the months that have expired up to that winter day when Max walked into my dressing-room. . . . When I was small and learning to knit, they made me undo rows and rows of stitches until I had found the little unnoticed fault, the dropped stitch, which at school was called "a lapse". A "lapse"! That's all that he would have been in my life, then, this poor second love of mine whom I used to call my dear warmth, my light. He is there, quite close at hand, I can take hold of him—and I flee.

For I shall flee. A premeditated escape is being organised far away, down in the depths of my being, without my taking so far any direct part in it. At the decisive moment, when all that remains will be to cry, as though in panic: "Quick, Blandine, my suitcase and a taxicab!" I shall perhaps be taken in by my own confusion, but O dear Max, whom I wanted to love, I confess here, with the most genuine sorrow, that from this moment all is resolved.

Except for this sorrow, have I not become again *what I was*, that is to say free, horribly alone and free? The momentary grace which touched me now withdraws itself from me, since I refused to lose myself in it. Instead of saying to it: "Take me!" I ask it: "What are you giving me? Another myself? There is no other myself. You're giving me a friend who is young, ardent, jealous and sincerely in love? I know: that is what is called a master, and I no longer want one. He is good and simple, he admires me and he is straightforward? In that case he is my inferior and I should be making a misalliance. A look of his can rouse me and I cease to belong to myself if he puts his mouth on mine? In that case he is my enemy, he is the thief who steals me from myself. I shall have everything, everything that money can buy, and I shall lean over the edge of

207

a white terrace smothered with the roses of my gardens? But it is from there that I shall see the lords of the earth, the wanderers, pass by! Come back to me, beseeches my love, leave your job and the shabby sadness of the surroundings where you live, come back among your equals. I have no equals, I have only my fellow wayfarers."

Windmills revolve on the horizon. In the little stations through which the train passes, Breton head-dresses, the first white head-dresses, blossom like daisies. Dazzled, I enter into the yellow kingdom of the brooms and the gorses. Gold, copper, and vermilion too—for the pale rape is there as well—set these poor heathlands ablaze with an unedurable light. I press my cheek and my outspread hands against the carriage windows, surprised not to feel it warm. We are crossing the conflagration, leagues and leagues of gorse in flower, wasted riches which rebuff even the goats, and where butterflies, made languorous by the warm scent like half-ripe peaches and pepper, flutter about with torn wings.

t h i r t e e n

A T CAEN, TWO DAYS BEFORE OUR RETURN, I FIND A LETTER from Max consisting of only one line, with no signature: "My Renée, do you no longer love me?"

That is all. I had not foreseen that gentleness and the simplicity of that question, which confound all my literature. What was it I wrote then, the last time?

That doesn't matter. If he loves me, it is not in my letters that he read the warning. If he loves me, he knows those mysterious shocks, that light, hurtful finger which strikes the heart, those small thunderbolts which suddenly arrest a gesture or cut short a burst of laughter. He knows that treason, desertion and lies can strike from a great way off, and he knows the brutality and infallibility of a *presentiment*.

Poor, poor friend that I wanted to love! You might have died, or deceived me, and I should have known nothing of it, I whom the best-hidden treachery wounded by telepathy once upon a time.

"My Renée, do you no longer love me?" I did not melt into passionate tears, but I jotted down on a sheet of paper the abbreviated message of a vaguely reassuring telegram: *"Shall be home five o'clock day after tomorrow. All love."*

I am subtly jealous of this man who is suffering. I re-read his complaint and talk to this letter as if I were speaking to him, with his firm mouth and angry eyebrows.

"You love and suffer and complain. That makes you just as I was when I was twenty. I am leaving you and, thanks to me, you may perhaps acquire what now you lack. Already you can see through protecting walls; does that not astonish you, you great, dense male? Nerves grown sensitive, an innocent, burning, suffering, hope for ever renewing itself, green and strong, like a mown field, all that was my portion and now it will be yours. I cannot take it away from you, but I begrudge it you."

There was a packet of letters with that of Max. Even Blandine writes: *"Madame, Monsieur Maxime has brought Fossette back, she has another new collar. Monsieur Maxime asks for news of Madame, he doesn't look very happy and one can see he's been missing Madame."*

There's a letter from Hamond, who talks simply but writes with an almost ceremonious courtesy; and a letter from Margot who has nothing to tell me and fills two sheets with a nun-like tittle-tattle. They are all in a hurry to write to me now I am about to return, as if their conscience were pricking them slightly for having neglected me for such a long time.

Whom shall I confide in when I get back? In Hamond? In Margot? In neither. I tear up all this trifling stuff before leaving the stifling tomb known as the "star's dressing-room" at the *Folies-Caennaises*, to go up on to the stage. We are in an old-style *café-chan-tant*: to reach the stage door one has to cross a part of the auditorium, and this is the worst moment of the evening. The public elbows us and bars our way on purpose so as to stare at us longer; my bare arm leaves its powder on a jacket, a hand slyly pulls at my embroidered shawl, and furtive fingers feel my hips. With heads high, we bear like proud prisoners the contempt and desire of this suffocating crowd.

fourteen

A HALF-HOUR STRIKES, VERY FAR AWAY. THE TRAIN FROM
Calais, which is to take me back to Paris, is not due for
fifty minutes.

I am returning alone, by night, without warning anyone.
Brague and the Old Troglodyte, their thirst slaked thanks to
me, are now asleep somewhere in Boulogne-sur-Mer. We
killed three-quarters of an hour in doing our accounts, and
chattering, and discussing plans for our South American tour,
and then I found myself in this station at Tintelleries, so deserted at this hour that one might think it was no longer in
use. They have not switched on the electric globes of the platform, just for me. A cracked bell tinkles timidly in the shadows, as though it were hanging from the neck of a paralysed
dog.

The night is cold and moonless. Near by, in an invisible
garden, there are scented lilacs which rustle in the wind. Far
away I can hear the call of foghorns at sea.

Who would guess that I am here, right at the end of the
platform, huddled in my coat? How well hidden I am! Neither
darker nor lighter than the shadows.

With the first light I shall let myself noiselessly into my flat,
like a thief, for I am not expected so soon. I shall wake Fossette and Blandine and then will come the hardest moment.

I deliberately imagine the details of my arrival; I conjure up,
with necessary cruelty, the memory of the twofold scent which
clings to the hangings: English tobacco and rather too-sweet

jasmine; in imagination I press the satin cushion with its two pale stains, the traces of two tears which fell from my eyes in a moment of very great happiness. I can hardly hold back the little stifled "ah!" of one who has been wounded and jolts her wound. I am doing it on purpose. It will hurt me less by and by.

From far away I am saying my goodbyes to all which would keep me there, and to him who will have nothing left of me, except a letter. A cowardly, rational wisdom persuades me not to see him again: no "frank explanations" between us! A heroine who is only human, like myself, is not strong enough to triumph over all the demons. Let him despise me and even curse me a little, it will be all the better if he does; poor dear, he'll recover more quickly. No, no, there mustn't be too much honesty. And not too many phrases either, since by keeping silent I shall spare him.

A man crosses the rails with sleepy steps, pushing a trunk on a hand-cart, and suddenly the electric globes of the station come on. I get up, feeling numb, I had not noticed I was very cold. At the end of the platform a lantern jerks in the darkness, swinging from an invisible arm. A distant whistle answers the harsh foghorns: it is the train. Already!

fifteen

"*GOODBYE, MY DARLING. I am going away, to a village not very far from here; after that I shall no doubt leave for America, with Brague. I shall not see you again, my darling. When you read this you will not think it is a cruel game, since the day before yesterday you wrote to me; 'My Renée, do you no longer love me?'*

"*I am going away, it is the least hurt I can do you. I am not cruel, Max, but I feel myself quite worn out, as though unable to resume the habit of loving and afraid lest I should have to suffer again because of it.*

"*You did not think I was so cowardly, my darling? What a small heart mine is! Yet once upon a time it could have been worthy of yours, which offers itself so simply. But now . . . what could I give you, oh my darling? In a few years' time the best of myself would be that frustrated maternity that a childless woman transfers to her husband. You do not accept that and neither do I. It is a pity. There are days when I, who watch myself growing older with a resigned terror, think of old age as a recompense.*

"*My darling, one day you will understand all this. You will understand that I must not belong to you or to anyone, and that in spite of a first marriage and a second love, I have remained a kind of old maid, like some among them who are so in love with Love that no love appears to them beautiful enough, and so they refuse themselves without condescending to explain; who repel every sentimental misalliance and return to sit for life before a window, bent over their*

*needle, in solitary communion with their incomparable vision. Like
them, I wanted everything; a lamentable mistake punished me.*

"*I no longer dare, my darling, that is the whole trouble, I no
longer dare. Don't be cross if I have hidden so long from you my
efforts to resuscitate in myself the enthusiasm, the adventurous fatalism, the blind hope, the whole cheerful escort of love. The only delir-
ium I feel is that of my senses. And alas, there is none whose intervals are more lucid. You would have consumed me to no purpose, you
whose gaze, whose lips, whose long caresses, whose moving silence
cured, for a little while, a distress which is not your fault.*

"*Goodbye, my darling. Seek far from me that youth, that fresh,
unspoilt beauty, that faith in the future and in yourself, in a word,
the love that you deserve, the love that once upon a time I could have
given you. Don't seek me out. I have just enough strength to flee
from you. If you were to walk in here, before me, while I am writing
to you . . . but you will not walk in.*

"*Goodbye, my darling. You are the one being in the world whom I
call my darling, and after you I have no one to whom to give that
name. For the last time, embrace me as if I were cold, hold me very
close, very close, very close. . . .*

Renée."

I have written very slowly; before signing my letter I re-read
it, rounded the loops, added the dots and the accents, and
dated it: *May 15th, 7 a.m.*

But though signed and dated and finally stuck down, it still
remains an unfinished letter. Shall I open it again? I suddenly
shiver as if, in closing the envelope, I had blocked out a luminous opening through which a warm breath of air was still
blowing.

It is a sunless morning and the winter cold seems to have
taken refuge in this little sitting-room behind the shutters that
have been padlocked for forty days. Crouching at my feet, my
dog is silent, her eyes on the door: she is waiting. She is waiting for someone who will not come again. I can hear Blandine

shifting the casseroles, I smell the smell of ground coffee; hunger gnaws sullenly at my stomach. A worn sheet covers the divan, a damp, blue mist tarnishes the mirror. I was not expected so soon. Everything is shrouded in old linen and dampness and dust, everything here still wears the slightly funereal air of departure and absence, and I pass furtively through this refuge of mine without taking off the white dust-sheets, without writing a name on the bloom of dust, without leaving any other trace of my passage than that letter, unfinished.

Unfinished. Dear intruder, whom I wanted to love, I spare you. By going away, I leave you your one chance of growing bigger in my eyes. Reading my letter will only give you pain. You will not know the humiliating comparison you are escaping, nor the dispute of which you were the prize, the prize which I disdain.

For I reject you and I choose . . . all that is not you. I have met you before, and I recognise you. Are you not he who, thinking he is giving, takes for himself? You came to share my life. To share, yes: *to take your share!* To be a partner in everything I do, to insinuate yourself at every moment in the secret temple of my thoughts, isn't that it? Why you, more than another? I have barred it to everyone.

You are good and, with the best faith in the world, you meant to bring me happiness, since you saw me deprived and solitary. But you counted without my beggar-woman's pride: I refuse to see the most beautiful countries of the world microscopically reflected in the amorous mirror of your eyes.

Happiness? Are you sure that happiness is enough for me henceforward? It is not only happiness that gives value to life. You wanted to brighten me with that commonplace dawn, for you pitied me in my obscurity. Call it obscurity, if you will: the obscurity of a room seen from without. I would rather call it dark, not obscure. Dark, but made beautiful by an unwearying sadness: silvery and twilit like the white owl, the silky mouse, the wings of the clothes-moth. Dark, with the red gleams of an agonising memory. But you are he in whose presence I should no longer have the right to be sad.

I escape from myself, but I am still not free of you, I know it. A vagabond, and free, I shall sometimes long for the shade of your walls. How many times shall I return to you, dear prop on which I rest and wound myself? How many times shall I cry for what you were able to give me: a long-drawn-out voluptuousness, suspended, fanned, renewed, the winged fall, the swooning in which one's strength is renewed by its own death . . . the musical drumming of the maddened blood . . . the scent of burning sandal-wood and trodden grass. . . . Ah, how long shall I not thirst for you upon my road!

I shall desire you as I desire in turn the fruit that hangs out of reach, the far-off water, and the blissful little house that I pass by. In each place where my desires have strayed, I leave thousands and thousands of shadows in my own shape, shed from me: one lies on the warm blue rocks of the ledges in my own country, another in the damp hollow of a sunless valley, and a third follows a bird, a sail, the wind and the wave. You keep the most enduring of them: a naked, undulating shadow, trembling with pleasure like a plant in the stream. But time will dissolve it like the others, and you will no longer know anything of me until the day when my steps finally halt and there will fly away from me a last small shadow.

About the Author

Sidonie Gabrielle Colette (1873–1954) was one of the most famous and honored French writers of this century. The first woman member of The Academie Goncourt, a holder of the Grand Cross of the Legion of Honor, she was also the first woman in French history to be granted a state funeral.

Colette began her writing career in collaboration with Willy, her husband. In 1900, when she was twenty-seven, Colette's first novel, *Claudine at School,* was published and became a sensational success. During the next few years, several *Claudine* books followed. After divorcing Willy, Colette earned her living as a music-hall mime, and in 1907, her first independent novel appeared, *Retreat from Love.*

With the outbreak of World War I, Colette began a career as a special correspondent in Rome and Venice and as a contributor to *Le Matin,* a leading Paris daily. Her journalism included dramatic criticism, law-court reporting, and sketches of contemporary life. During this time, Colette continued to write novels.

During her last years, Colette, crippled by arthritis and confined to her Paris apartment, wrote reminiscences and descriptive works that gained her new renown. Before her death in 1954, at the age of eighty-one, Colette had written more than fifty books and was best known as the creator of *Gigi, Chéri* and *The Last of Chéri,* and the *Claudine* novels. Among her countrymen, her place in twentieth-century fiction is comparable to that of Proust.